"Hurry, Julia. We don't have much time."

Abraham held out his hand to her. Fear flashed in Julia's eyes. Abraham's heart went out to her for the situation they were in. All she wanted to do was keep her son safe, yet they were walking into the middle of a clash between two street gangs. They were taking a big risk that could turn deadly.

"We have to keep going." Abraham put his hand on Julia's shoulder and guided her forward. She scooted William closer toward Abraham so the boy would be protected between them.

"We'll slip out along the side of the road," Abraham said. "Act nonchalant." They stayed on the sidewalk, keeping their eyes averted so they would not make eye contact.

"Hey, you!" someone shouted.

"They must have seen us!"

* * *

Amish Witness Protection

Amish Hideout by Maggie K. Black—January 2019
Amish Safe House by Debby Giusti—February 2019
Amish Haven by Dana R. Lynn—March 2019

Debby Giusti is an award-winning Christian author who met and married her military husband at Fort Knox, Kentucky. Together they traveled the world, raised three wonderful children and have now settled in Atlanta, Georgia, where Debby spins tales of mystery and suspense that touch the heart and soul. Visit Debby online at debbygiusti.com, blog with her at seekerville.Blogspot.com and craftieladiesofromance.Blogspot.com, and email her at Debby@DebbyGiusti.com.

Books by Debby Giusti

Love Inspired Suspense

Amish Witness Protection

Amish Safe House

Amish Protectors

Amish Refuge
Undercover Amish
Amish Rescue
Amish Christmas Secrets

Military Investigations

The Soldier's Sister
The Agent's Secret Past
Stranded
Person of Interest
Plain Danger
Plain Truth

Visit the Author Profile page at Harlequin.com for more titles.

AMISH SAFE HOUSE

DEBBY GIUSTI

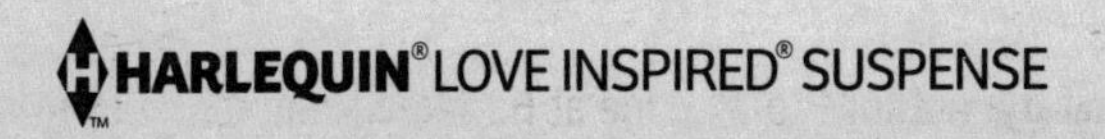

Special thanks and acknowledgment are given to Debby Giusti for her contribution to the Amish Witness Protection series.

ISBN-13: 978-1-335-23189-5

Amish Safe House

This edition published by arrangement with Love Inspired Books.

www.Harlequin.com

Printed in U.S.A.

Trust in the Lord with all thine heart;
and lean not unto thine own understanding. In all
thy ways acknowledge him, and he shall direct thy paths.
—*Proverbs* 3:5-6

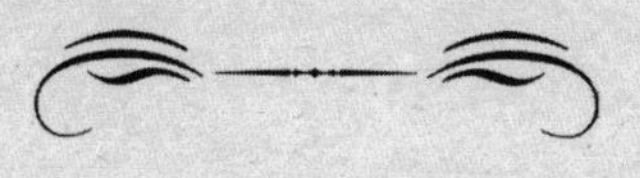

To our law enforcement heroes.

May God bless them and keep them in His care.

PROLOGUE

Gunfire!

Julia Bradford's pulse raced. "Kayla, where's your brother?"

"He took out the trash."

Julia rinsed the plate she was washing and glanced at the overflowing trash bag still on the floor by the kitchen counter, then peered through the window at the dumpster in the empty alleyway below.

Another round of gunshots. Her heart thumped a warning. She wiped her hand on a dish towel and hurried into the living area. "When did he leave?"

Her seven-year-old daughter clutched her doll and shrugged. Thankfully, Kayla seemed oblivious to the gang warfare that held this part of the inner city hostage.

"Come with me." Julia reached for her daughter's hand.

Kayla reluctantly rose from the floor, still holding her doll, and slipped her small hand into her mother's. "Where are we going?"

"To Mrs. Fielding's apartment."

Kayla's face broke into a wide smile. "Maybe she baked cookies today."

If only all of life's problems could be solved with a cookie.

"Hurry." Julia ushered her daughter into the stairwell and up one flight of steps.

She knocked on the apartment door. "Mrs. Fielding?"

Relieved when the sweet neighbor with the warm gaze and understanding smile opened the door, Julia gently guided Kayla through the doorway.

"William's outside," she explained. "I heard gunshots."

The older woman's brown eyes widened. "Lord, protect that boy."

"Can you watch Kayla?"

"Of course, dear."

"Lock the door, Mrs. Fielding. The gangs have started following their victims into stairwells."

"God help us." The woman moaned as she pointed Kayla toward the table. "Sit there, baby. I'll get you a cookie."

Once the door closed, Julia waited to hear the click of the dead bolt fall into place before she raced down the stairs, pushed on the outer door and stepped into the cool night air.

A *pop-pop-pop* sounded, followed by a rapid burst of semiautomatic gunfire. Heart in her throat, Julia ran toward the sound.

"William?" She glanced into the alley, the neighboring apartment, the small grocery on the corner with its windows barred to stop the rampant crime.

"Thank you, Charlie," Julia spat out, her hands fisted. Anger at her ex-husband bubbled up anew.

More gunfire, peppered with angry shouts.

Where's Will?

She turned left at the intersection, then right onto a side street. Her gut tightened. Halfway down the block two bodies lay sprawled on the roadway. Dark swaths of blood pooled on the pavement.

Fear tangled her spine.

William!

She wanted to scream his name, but her outcry would draw attention to a fourteen-year-old enamored of punk teens and twentysomethings who flaunted knives and guns and endless cash.

She blamed Charlie, her ex, who was serving time. So much for fatherly love. The only thing he had provided for his children was a heritage of crime.

Slipping into a nearby alleyway, she peered at the thugs marked with tattoos and piercings milling around their fallen comrades.

More shots. A man gasped, his face caught in the headlights of an oncoming car. He clutched his chest and collapsed to the pavement. Just that quickly, the rival gangs scattered.

Footsteps sounded. Julia held her breath and narrowed her gaze, trying to determine who was approaching.

Her eyes widened.

William!

She stepped from the darkness and grabbed her son's hand. "Where were you?"

"Mom, please." He jerked free.

"You snuck out."

"I told Kayla."

"You didn't tell me."

She glanced back. Three men stood staring at them. Julia's heart lurched. She motioned William forward. "Go home. Now."

Footsteps slapped the pavement behind them. She turned again. Her heart stopped. The men were running toward them.

"Hurry, Will."

With his long legs and easy gait, her son moved ahead

of her. They turned left at the corner and right at the next intersection. Her lungs burned. She gasped for air.

William climbed the stairs to their apartment building and plugged in the code. The door clicked open. He disappeared into the stairwell.

Julia followed him inside and up the stairs. He stood at the door of their apartment, fumbling with the key.

Shouts sounded below.

"Where is he?" Male voices. "Where's that punk kid? David's friend. He saw it all go down."

Another voice, coming from the same group. "I know his apartment number. Follow me."

Heavy footfalls pounded the stairs.

Julia's heart stopped. She reached around William and jiggled the key. The door to their apartment opened. She shoved him into the living room, slammed the door behind her and engaged the lock.

"Hide, Will. In the bathroom."

She grabbed her cell phone off a side table and followed her son through the bedroom to the bath beyond, locking both doors behind them just as the gang members crashed through the front door and entered the apartment.

"Lay down." She motioned William into the tub. "Cover your head with your hands."

Trembling, Julia punched 911 into her cell. "The Philador gang," she said, breathless, once the operator answered. "Three of them…in my apartment."

She gave the address, the words spilling out one after another. "My son and I…locked in the bath. Hurry."

Angry shouts. Glass shattered. A heavy object clattered to the floor.

God, can You hear me? Protect my child.

Julia pushed her weight against the bathroom door, hoping it would hold. Her heart raced. A roar filled her ears.

If only the police…

Sirens sounded.

Would they get there in time?

Voices in the bedroom. Something or someone rammed the bathroom door.

"You're dead, punk."

William glanced up, his face twisted with fear.

Another crash to the door.

She thought of her daughter with Mrs. Fielding in the upstairs apartment.

Keep them safe.

"Police!" a voice shouted.

A shot, followed in a nanosecond by another. A scream. Then the scurry of feet.

Someone pounded on the door. "Ma'am, it's the police. Unlock the door."

Could she trust the voice? Could she trust anyone?

Will climbed from the tub, his cheeks wet with tears, his nose running. He touched her hand.

She saw his lips move, but she couldn't understand what he was saying.

He nudged her aside, undid the lock and slowly opened the door.

Hands grabbed both of them and pulled them through the bedroom, past two bleeding bodies on the floor, past the group of officers huddled around another gang member. His wrists were cuffed behind his back. Curly black hair, a mustache and goatee, deep-set eyes that stared at her as they passed.

Recognition flickered in the back of Julia's mind.

A female officer introduced herself and held up a badge. "We're taking you someplace safe."

Julia shook her head. She reached for William and pulled him close. "My son?"

"He's going with you."

"Kayla? My…my daughter—"

"Where is she, ma'am?"

"Upstairs."

Without letting go of William's hand, Julia climbed the stairs, pulling her son behind her. The officer followed.

"It's Julia." She tapped on Mrs. Fielding's door. "I need my daughter."

The door cracked open. Mrs. Fielding peered through the narrow crevice.

"Where's Kayla?"

"Mama!" The child yanked on the door. Her eyes widened as she glanced at the throng of police swarming the stairwell. "What's wrong, Mama?"

Julia pointed to the female officer. "We're going someplace with this lady."

"I don't wanna go."

"Shhh, Kayla. It'll be okay."

"My dolly."

"Kayla, please."

She ran back into the apartment and returned with the doll clutched in her arms.

Julia squeezed Mrs. Fielding's hand. "Thank you."

"God keep you safe," the older woman said. "I'm praying for you."

If only God would listen.

The officer touched Julia's arm. "We need to leave now."

"My purse?"

"I'll have someone retrieve your things."

"I homeschool my children. There are books and—"

"I'll tell them to bring the schoolbooks and supplies." The officer put her hand on Julia's shoulder and pointed her down the stairs.

Outside, the flashing lights of the ambulance and police

squad cars captured them in their glare. Julia pulled her children close and ran toward the waiting car, her head lowered as the officer had instructed.

They slid into the back seat of the large sedan. Heat pumped from air vents. Julia buckled seat belts and wrapped her arms around the children, her heart nearly pounding out of her chest.

The officer glanced at William. "Did you see anyone shot this evening?"

He lowered his gaze and nodded. "Oscar… Oscar de la Rosa."

"Who shot him?"

William glanced at Julia before he answered, his voice little more than a whisper. "Frankie Fuentes."

Julia's heart broke. Her son was caught in the middle of a Philadelphia turf war between the Philadores and Delphis. Both gangs killed in cold blood and left no witnesses.

Kayla snuggled closer, her eyes heavy.

"Everything's all right, sweetie," Julia assured her.

But it wasn't. Nothing was right and everything was wrong.

ONE

"I have your new identities." US Marshal Jonathan Mast sat across the table from Julia in the hotel, situated on the outskirts of Philadelphia, where she and her children had been holed up for the last five days. He was a pensive man with a dark beard and equally dark eyes.

"The night of the shooting I asked you to be patient, Mrs. Bradford, and you have been, which we all appreciate." He glanced at the two other marshals at the table. Both Stacy Porter, slender and focused on her job, and Karl Adams, more laid-back with an easy smile, nodded in agreement.

Julie didn't feel patient. She felt frustrated and stir-crazy. Keeping her children content in a two-room suite had been a challenge. Plus, she was scared to death about their safety.

The Philadores wanted to kill William so he wouldn't testify against their leader. As much as Julia didn't trust law enforcement, she had to rely on the US Marshals and their witness protection program to keep her family safe. No wonder her nerves were stretched thin. She had slept little over the last four nights, and the nagging headache and dark circles under her eyes were proof of her struggle to maintain some semblance of normalcy in her children's lives.

As efficient as Marshal Mast seemed, he failed to realize how antsy kids could be without sunshine and fresh air. Fortunately, Stacy and Karl had seemed more empathetic. Both in their early thirties, they had played games with William and Kayla and had provided pizza and colas and an abundance of snacks. But even a diet of junk food got old.

"We're ready to transport you and the children," Jonathan Mast continued. "We'll fly into Kansas City tonight, then drive to Topeka and north to Yoder."

"What's in Kansas?"

"What's *not* there is more important. Kansas is one of the few states where the Philadores don't have a strong presence. As I've mentioned previously, Frankie Fuentes is a killer. He runs drugs, has his hand in prostitution, trafficking and illegal gambling. Three weeks ago, he gunned down two cops in cold blood. No witnesses and no way to bring him to justice. Your son saw him kill Oscar de la Rosa. William's testimony will send Fuentes to jail for a long time."

Jonathan pulled out his phone and accessed a photograph. He handed the cell to Julia. "Abraham King will watch over you in Kansas."

Julia studied the picture. The man looked to be in his midthirties with a square face and deep-set eyes beneath dark brows. His nose appeared a bit off center, as if it had been broken. Lips pulled tight, and no hint of a smile on his angular face.

"Mr. King doesn't look happy."

Jonathan shrugged. "Law enforcement photos are never flattering."

Her stomach tightened. "He's a cop?"

"Past tense. He left the force three years ago."

Once a cop, always a cop. Her ex had been a police officer. He protected others but failed to show that same sense of concern when it came to his own family. After Charlie, she wanted nothing to do with men in uniform.

The marshal seemed oblivious to her unease.

"Abe is an old friend," Jonathan continued. "A widower from my police-force days who owns a farm and has a spare house on his property. He lives in a rural Amish community."

"Amish?"

"That's right."

"Bonnets and buggies?" she asked.

He smiled weakly. "You'll be off the grid, Mrs. Bradford. No one will look for you there. If anyone asks, you'll be working as Abraham's housekeeper, at least until the trial."

"Has a date been set?"

"Not yet. Everything takes time."

Julia tried to get her mind around a new identity in a new state. She didn't understand the Amish connection, but she was okay with anything that meant William and Kayla would be safe.

"My ex-husband..."

She glanced into the adjoining bedroom where William was watching a sporting event on ESPN. Kayla stood nearby and pretended to feed her doll.

Julia lowered her voice. "My ex-husband won't know of our whereabouts?"

"That's correct."

"He won't be able to find us," she repeated, needing the reassurance she hoped the marshal would provide.

"No one will find you, ma'am."

"William will be safe in Kansas?"

"Yes, ma'am."

"As you probably know, my husband was a cop." She glanced again at the photo. "I'm... I'm hesitant to rely on someone with that background. Do you know why Mr. King was forced to resign?"

Jonathan stiffened. "Abraham had a stellar record with law enforcement, Mrs. Bradford."

"I didn't mean to imply…" She held up her hand. "I'm just worried about the safety of my children. They come first."

"Of course they do, but let me assure you, their safety, as well as yours, is our top priority."

He retrieved his phone from her outstretched hand and tucked it into his pocket. "Abraham put a criminal in jail who wanted payback after he was paroled. The guy planted an explosive device in Abe's car. The next morning, his wife tried to drive their daughter to daycare. The car exploded, and his wife and four-year-old child were killed."

The marshal's matter-of-fact disclosure of the tragedy hit Julia hard. She glanced down at the table, fighting back tears that welled up in her eyes at the senseless loss of life. "I'm sorry."

Jonathan nodded. "It was a tough time for him, as you can imagine."

"Did Mr. King agree to shelter us?"

"He did. Your identities and location will probably change again after William testifies, but for now, you'll be Julia Stolz."

"A German name."

"Yes, ma'am. The area has a large German as well as Amish population. Stolz will fit in."

"I don't speak German."

"That won't be a problem." He pulled a manila folder from his briefcase and placed it on the table in front of her. "Here's the paperwork you need for your new identities. Social security cards with new names and numbers for you and the children. Birth certificates. A high school graduation diploma for Julia Stolz."

Jonathan glanced into the bedroom. "William and Kayla need to understand the importance of not revealing their old identities."

Kayla wouldn't be a problem, but William was going through a defiant stage where he rebelled against everything.

As if reading her mind, Mast added, "William needs to know that his safety as well as yours and your daughter's depends on him agreeing to this new life."

Julia nodded. "I'll talk to him."

But would he listen?

Pushing his chair back from the table, Jonathan glanced at his fellow marshals. "We'll leave at nine tonight."

"Why so late?" Julia asked.

"At the present time, the Philadores don't know your whereabouts. We don't want that to change." He stood. "Stacy and Karl will drive you to the airport. I'll meet you there."

True to his word, Marshal Mast was waiting on the tarmac when Karl pulled the sedan to a stop next to the small charter plane that night.

Julia and her children were ushered onboard. Kayla fell asleep not long after the plane was airborne. William nodded off soon thereafter. Julia stared out the window, peering into the dark sky. Her head throbbed, her eyes burned and she was cold, too cold.

Stacy handed her blankets. "You've been very brave."

Julia covered her children and herself with the blankets and almost laughed. Not brave, but maybe foolish to think she could outsmart the Philadores. Her eyes closed. The jerk of the plane when the wheels touched down forced them open again.

"We've landed." Stacy patted Julia's arm. "A van will take us to your final destination."

Julia ushered her children off the plane and into the vehicle parked on the tarmac.

Karl slipped behind the wheel. Jonathan sat in the passenger's seat, and Stacy climbed into the rear.

Kayla fell asleep again, her head on Julia's lap. William leaned against her shoulder. Soon, he too drifted off.

Julia watched the lights of the city fade from view as they headed into the country. She quickly lost track of the twists and turns in the road and slipped into a half sleep.

A hand tapped her shoulder. "We're almost to our destination."

The car turned off the paved road onto a dirt drive that led to a two-story house with a porch and overhanging tin roof. A small light glowed in a downstairs window.

A second house, similar in style but a bit larger, sat not more than twenty feet away.

Stacy slipped out from the rear. "I'll carry Kayla." She lifted the girl into her arms.

"William, wake up." Julia patted her son's arm. "We're going inside."

He rubbed his eyes and followed her out of the van. Julia took Kayla from the marshal and then grabbed William's hand, surprised that he didn't balk. Most days, he objected to any show of affection.

Julia's stomach churned. She hugged Kayla closer and gripped her son's hand more tightly as they followed Stacy up the steps to the porch.

The door opened. A man stood backlit on the threshold. "You made good time," he said in greeting.

"No traffic this late at night." Marshal Mast extended his hand. The two men shook, then embraced in a backslapping half-hug of sorts that confirmed the friendship Jonathan had mentioned.

The homeowner shook hands with the two other marshals and invited them inside. "There's coffee. I placed ham and cheese and bread on the table, in case you're hungry."

He glanced at her and nodded. "Ma'am."

Stepping inside, she narrowed her gaze and studied the sparse accommodations. A table, sideboard, a wood-burning stove. Glancing into another room, she saw two rockers, a bench, a chest of drawers and another table.

She focused again on the man who had welcomed them to his house. He wore a white shirt and trousers held up with suspenders. No collar on the shirt. No buttons. No belt. Work boots scuffed with mud. Turning she saw the pegs on the wall by the door and the black, wide-brimmed felt hat and the short black waistcoat.

She glanced at the marshals who were pouring coffee and helping themselves to the bread and cold cuts on the table. The only person who noticed her discomfort was the man whose photo she had seen earlier today. His deep-set eyes stared at her as if questioning why she was there.

Julia wanted to ask the same question. Jonathan had mentioned that Abraham was living Amish, but the stark reality of what that meant hit her like a sledgehammer. No phone, no electrical power, no technology. *Off the grid,* as Jonathan had mentioned, was an understatement. Plus, the Amish were pacifists. If they didn't believe in violence or raising a hand against another, then what if the Philadores discovered where she and her children were hiding?

Her heart sank as she looked at the tall man with the questioning gaze. A former cop who didn't fit the law enforcement model. No matter what Jonathan claimed, she didn't see how Abraham King could protect her and her children if he was Amish.

Abraham had made a mistake. As much as he owed Jonathan, he never should have agreed to bring a woman into his life.

Losing everyone he had ever loved had taken him to the brink of despair. Jonathan had saved him and brought him back to life, a life of hard work and isolation. A life without a woman to stir up memories of Marianne and their precious little girl, Becca. His breath caught as he thought of the pain that never seemed to end.

Surely Jonathan would understand if Abraham backed out of their agreement. Then he glanced at Julia. Too thin, too afraid, too lost. He knew the signs of a person holding on by a whisper. He had been that person three years ago.

The boy standing next to her was tall and gangly, as if a growth spurt had caught him unawares. His brown eyes, like his mother's, peered warily at the three marshals gathered around the table. The kid looked tired and confused and ready to bolt if given the chance.

"His dad's doing time," Jonathan had shared. "Wouldn't take much for the kid to follow in his father's footsteps from what we know. You're the family's last hope, Abraham."

Abraham sighed. How could he turn his back on a woman and two children in such need?

"The bedrooms are upstairs." Abraham stepped toward her. "I can show you the way. Perhaps the children would like to go to sleep."

"I'm sure they would." Clutching her daughter in her arms, she nodded to her son, and the weary threesome followed Abraham up the stairs.

Carrying an oil lamp to light the way, he chastised

himself for not placing a lit lamp in each of the bedrooms. Darkness could be frightening, especially to children in new surroundings.

He opened the first door on the right. "I thought your daughter could sleep here."

The woman hesitated a moment and stared at the furnishings. A single bed, small dresser, and a side table with a water pitcher and basin.

She moved into the room, pulled back the covers and laid her little girl on the bed. Quickly, she removed Kayla's shoes and covered her with a quilt.

Abraham glanced down at the child's blond hair and chubby cheeks. A knife stabbed his heart as Becca's face filled his vision. He turned away and headed to the door.

"William, your mother will sleep across the hall. The room next door is for you." Thankfully, the boy followed.

"I will leave the lamp in the hallway."

"You…you don't have electricity?" the boy asked, his voice filled with wonder.

"We use oil lamps."

The boy frowned.

Abraham stepped back into the hallway to give the lad privacy as he untied his shoes and got ready for bed.

Julia stepped past him and entered the room. She pulled the covers around her son's shoulders and brushed the hair from his forehead. "Go to sleep, William. We'll talk tomorrow. I'll be across the hall."

"I don't wanna stay here."

She nodded. "I know."

The boy's eyes closed and he was soon asleep.

Abraham placed the lamp on a small table in the hallway. Julia joined him there.

"I appreciate you taking us in, Mr. King."

"Please, my name is Abraham. Some call me Abe."

"I hate to disturb your life, but Marshal Mast—"

"You have disturbed nothing, Ms. Stolz."

Her brow wrinkled.

"Perhaps Jonathan did not provide your new name?"

"He did. It's just that..." She raked her hand through her golden-brown hair. "So much has happened."

"We can review the information you will need tomorrow."

"Thank you, Abraham." She glanced into her room and then hurried downstairs.

The marshals were eating sandwiches and finishing their coffee. They stood when she entered the kitchen.

Stacy pointed to a plastic bag sitting next to the luggage by the door. "I brought a few games for the kids."

Julia offered a weak smile. "That was very thoughtful."

"William and Kayla will adjust." Stacy squeezed her arm. "You will, too."

"I hope so."

Jonathan shook hands with Abraham. "Thanks for the chow."

"You are traveling back to Philadelphia tonight?"

"We'll be at our desks before dawn." The marshal turned to Julia. "You can call us if you need anything. Abraham's neighbor has a phone. Do you have any questions?"

"None that I can think of at the moment."

The marshals shook her hand and then left the house. Stacy and Karl climbed into the van. Jonathan hung back.

"I'll leave the coded message on your neighbor's answering machine if anything new develops," he told Abraham, who had followed them outside. "Let me know if you notice anything suspicious. The Philadores don't have much of a foothold in Kansas, but that could change."

He slapped Abraham's shoulder. "Nice seeing you, Abe. Looks like you've settled into Amish life."

"Coming back was a good decision for me." Abraham hesitated. "I will always be grateful."

"You saved my hide a few times. The least I could do was reciprocate."

Jonathan glanced back at the house before adding, "I know this is hard, but the kid's in danger. I don't have to tell you the woman looks fragile and at the end of her rope. The boy could be the biggest problem. The cops in Philly found him on the street a couple times and took him home. The mom's trying hard, but we both know sometimes that's not good enough. Plus, her ex-husband came after her following their divorce. She got a restraining order and changed locations twice. Each time he found her. He eventually went to prison, but he talked about getting even. She's carrying a lot of worry, especially concerning her son. Maybe you can redirect the kid and focus him on something other than gangs and crime."

"The Amish way is not for everyone, Jonathan. You know that."

"*Yah*." The marshal slipped into his own Amish roots. "But for a kid who doesn't know where to turn, the hard work and strong sense of community might give him a new outlook on life. As I mentioned when I first contacted you, my wife was in WitSec and was placed within the Amish community, which proved successful. I have confidence you'll make this work as well, Abraham."

"When I agreed to help, I thought there would be a husband." Abraham tugged on his jaw. "A husband who would follow his wife here at some later time, instead of an ex locked away in prison."

"I may have skipped over that detail."

Abraham chuckled. "You knew I would never agree to a woman without a husband."

"You'll be in the house next door."

"Of course I will, but she was hurt by her ex and probably struggles to trust men."

"Wouldn't you struggle, if you had been through what she has? Her husband had a passion for gambling. Too much debt and to the wrong people. Then he embezzled funds to cover his habit."

"Being placed with a female might have been a better fit."

"Encourage her to call Stacy if she needs to talk to another woman. In the meantime, you're our man on this case, Abe. The family needs you."

Again the two men shook hands. As Jonathan turned toward the car, his cell rang. He pulled it out, pushed Talk and raised the phone to his ear. "Mast." He nodded. "You're sure? Thanks. I'll pass that on."

Pocketing his phone, Jonathan turned worried eyes to Abraham. "We picked up an informant who was eager to talk. Fuentes got wind of us moving William out of Philadelphia."

"How?"

Jonathan shrugged. "Beats me, but it compounds the situation. Not that they suspect Kansas. Still, stay alert. His people could be anywhere and anyone."

"Are you sure the informant is legit?"

"As sure as we can be. I'll call you if we get more information."

Jonathan hurried to the van and climbed into the front seat. The three marshals nodded their farewells before the vehicle drove away, leaving Abraham to think of the family he had not been able to protect.

His own family.

He turned and, with a heavy heart, entered the kitchen. The woman stood by the table.

"I live in the house next door," he said. "I will leave you to your rest now. Tomorrow we will talk about this new arrangement."

He touched the dead bolt on the kitchen door. "The front door is locked. Do the same with the dead bolt once I leave. Do not worry. The only person prowling the grounds tonight will be me. I will not let harm come to you or your children."

Without waiting for her to comment, Abraham grabbed his hat and coat from the wall pegs and stepped outside.

He paused and listened for the door to lock.

Silence.

He knocked. "Lock the door, Mrs. Stolz, for your own peace of mind."

The lock clicked into place. With a heavy sigh, he headed home.

He was glad he had bought the main house and the *dawdy*, or grandparents' house, next door. Abraham had not needed two houses, but he had wanted the land. One hundred twenty acres to farm and to exhaust him so he would forget about Marianne and Becca. Except he could never forget his wife and child.

Now this woman had stepped into his quiet world with her two children and all he could think about was what he had lost.

He had made a mistake agreeing to help Jonathan. In a few days Abraham would tell him the setup was not working and insist he find somewhere else to place Julia and her children.

Abraham kicked a clod of dirt with his boot and sighed, knowing that if the Philador gang was after them, there would be no place safe for Julia and her children to hide.

TWO

Julia awoke to someone pounding on the door.

She blinked her eyes open to see a blue curtain covering the bedroom window and tried to remember where she was.

Not the apartment in Philly.

Kansas.

Her heart sank. For a moment, she had hoped everything had been a dream.

Rising from the bed, she slipped into her jeans and pulled on the sweater she had worn last night. Hunger nagged at her stomach and made her hurry that much faster down the stairs. She wanted the children to sleep in, at least until she'd had a cup of coffee.

Another rap sounded at the kitchen door. She glanced out the window, relieved to see the tall Amish man standing on the porch. She raked her hair out of her face, twisted the lock and pulled open the door.

Her breath hitched. She hadn't realized how tall he was or how muscular. She pulled the sweater across her chest and took a step back, needing to distance herself from his bulk and his pensive eyes that stared down at her.

He held out a large ceramic mug. "Coffee?"

In his other hand, he held a jug of milk that he gave

her. "There's sugar in the kitchen. Breakfast will be ready in fifteen minutes."

"The children are still asleep."

"Wake them so they can eat."

"I wanted to let them sleep."

"Chores need to be done."

"Chores?"

He nodded. "A farm does not run on its own. To eat, we must work."

She glanced around his broad chest and scanned the surrounding area. Horses grazed in a nearby pasture. Cattle waited at a feed trough in the distance.

"Okay," she said. "We'll see you in fifteen minutes."

"*Gut.*" He turned and headed back to his house.

Julia inhaled the rich aroma of the coffee, added a dollop of milk and sighed with the first sip. Strong and hot, just the way she liked it.

Turning back to the kitchen, she spied a wooden box and opened the lid, seeing the insulation and feeling the coolness. She bent to examine a trap door that she slid open to find a chunk of ice.

"Who needs electricity?" She placed the milk in the aluminum-lined icebox and then tugged their suitcases upstairs. She rummaged through the contents until she found her toiletries.

Using the water in the pitcher, she washed her face and hands and brushed her teeth, then pulled her hair into a knot at the base of her neck.

Taking another sip of coffee, she knocked on William's open door and stepped toward the bed. "Time to get up, sleepyhead."

She brushed her hand over his hair, wishing he could always be so calm and peaceful. "Abraham is fixing breakfast. I'm sure you're hungry."

William opened one eye. "That big dude cooks?"

Julia tried to squelch a smile. "That dude is named Abraham. I have a feeling he can do a lot of things, and it sounds as though if you miss breakfast, you won't eat until lunch."

Both eyes opened. "Okay. I'm outta here."

"I put a clean shirt on the chair. There's water in the pitcher. Pour it into the basin to wash your hands and face and brush your teeth."

"Rules, Mom. Too many."

No doubt their host would have more rules for them to follow.

Kayla woke with a smile and hopped out of bed without needing to be told twice. She slipped into a fresh blouse and jeans and reached for her doll, tucked under the quilt. "I hope Mr. Abraham makes something good for breakfast. My tummy is hungry."

"Whatever he prepares will be appreciated, Kayla. Be sure to say please and thank you."

"I always remember even if Will doesn't."

"You set a good example for your brother."

The child smiled as if they shared a secret. Julia brushed Kayla's hair and helped her wash her face. "You look lovely."

Hand in hand, they headed downstairs, where William waited in the kitchen. "It's weird, Mom."

"What is?"

"The fridge looks like a box cooled with a big chunk of ice."

"That's what it is, Will. An icebox. The Amish don't use electricity."

"That's crazy."

"Maybe to you, but many people enjoy the *plain* life as it's called."

"Plain and stupid," Will grumbled under his breath. Julia chose to ignore the remark as she pulled open the kitchen door and guided the children into the cool springtime morning.

The musky smell of the rich soil and fresh air greeted them. She peered at the sun, which was peeking through an overcast sky. A crow cawed from the branches of a gnarled oak in the front yard. The irony wasn't lost on her. For so long, she had yearned to live in the country where the air wasn't stagnant with car exhaust and a crowd of buildings didn't block the sun. Strange that her son being caught in the middle of a gang war would lead them to this remote Amish farm.

Then she thought of the Philadores, who wouldn't give up their search until they found William. Narrowing her gaze, she stared at the distant road where a pickup truck traveled well over the speed limit. Someone local, no doubt, yet instinctively, she put her arm around Will's shoulder and pulled him close.

God, if you're listening, protect my child.

He shrugged out of her hold just as the door to the nearby house opened and Abraham stepped onto the porch.

"I had planned to ring the dinner bell to summon you," he said, his voice warm with welcome. "Your timing is perfect. Breakfast is on the table."

Kayla ran ahead and climbed the stairs. "I'm hungry, Mr. Abraham."

"What about your dolly?" Abraham asked, eyeing the doll she clutched in her arm.

Kayla smiled. "She's hungry, too."

"Does she have a name?"

"Marianne. My daddy gave her to me."

Abraham's face clouded. He glanced at Julia, pain visible in his gaze.

"Mr. Abraham might not want a doll at the breakfast table," Julia said to ease his upset. Then, fearing they may have offended his faith, she added, "As I recall, Amish dolls don't have faces, although I'm not sure why."

"It has to do with graven images, but only in certain communities." Abraham held up his hand. "Having a doll with a face is not a problem here in Yoder."

He glanced down at Kayla and smiled. "If you do not mind, I will call your doll Annie."

The child shrugged. "That's a pretty name, too."

"What do you and Annie usually eat for breakfast?" he asked.

Kayla scrunched up her sweet face. "Mom makes us eat oatmeal."

"Does she?" He laughed, and the pain evaporated. "It appears from your expression that you do not like oatmeal."

"Oatmeal's okay and it's cheap. That's why we eat it."

"Kayla May, you don't need to bore Mr. King with our family's financial situation."

He held the door open and motioned them inside.

A man's house. Sparse but tidy. Two wooden rockers sat near the wood-burning stove in the middle of the room. A long table with chairs on one side and a bench by the wall divided the kitchen from the living area. A hutch and sideboard sat in the kitchen, a blanket chest and bookshelf in the larger living area.

Blue curtains, just as in the smaller house, were pulled back from the windows, a cloth covered the table, and oil lamps sat on a shelf in the kitchen.

"Sit on the bench, children," he directed. "Your mother can take the chair across from me."

"May I help serve the food?" she asked.

"Everyone likes pancakes?" He raised a brow.

Kayla's eyes widened. "I do."

"William, what about you?"

He shrugged. "They're okay."

"I also scrambled eggs and fried some slices of ham." Abraham handed Julia a plate. "Give the children as much as they can eat."

While she put pancakes and a slice of ham on each plate along with a spoonful of scrambled eggs, Abraham poured milk for the children and coffee for the adults.

He held her chair, which she hadn't expected. How long had it been since anyone had done that for her?

Shaking off the memory of Charlie on one of their first dates, she slid onto the chair and placed her napkin on her lap.

William reached for his fork. She held up her hand, waiting as Abraham sat and bowed his head. Eyeing her son, she nodded for him to follow Abraham's lead and hoped both children would remember how to give thanks.

Not that God would be listening to Julia's prayer. Still, she was grateful. *Keep us safe*, she thought before grabbing a fork and lifting a portion of the sweet and savory pancake into her mouth.

"Breakfast is delicious," she said between bites.

William, usually a picky eater, gobbled down everything on his plate and asked for more.

Abraham nodded his approval. "You have a good appetite, *yah*?"

Will wrinkled his brow and chuckled. "*Yah*."

Julia frowned at her son. She was grateful Abraham either hadn't realized or chose to ignore William's disrespect.

Once they had eaten, she helped Abraham clear the

table. "I can wash the dishes. You mentioned having chores to do."

"The soap is under the sink." He grabbed a hat hanging on a wall peg. "Come with me, William. We need to feed the neighbor's livestock."

The boy hesitated.

"William," he called again.

Slowly, the boy rose and shuffled to the door.

Abraham grabbed a basket from the sideboard. "Kayla, you can gather eggs."

"What about Annie?"

He smiled. "Annie should stay inside and help your mother with the dishes."

Satisfied with the response, Kayla sat the doll on a chair and hurried after Abraham.

"Is gathering eggs like an Easter egg hunt, Mr. Abraham?"

"Perhaps a bit. I will show you." He motioned the child toward the door and then glanced at Julia. "After Kayla collects the eggs, she will return to the house. Then William and I will go to the farm across the road. Harvey Raber and his sons are delivering the furniture they make to customers who placed orders. The neighbors lend a hand while they are gone."

Julia glanced quickly around the tidy kitchen and peered into the living area. "Shall I start cleaning?"

"You are a housekeeper in name only, Julia. You and Kayla can return to your house. I am sure you have things to do there."

She appreciated his thoughtfulness. "I'd like to unpack."

"Lock the door. If there is a problem, ring the dinner bell. I will hear you."

In spite of the peaceful setting and Abraham's attempt

to welcome them to farm life, his mention of using a bell if she or Kayla had a problem, made the anxiety Julia had felt in Philadelphia return. She and the children had traveled over a thousand miles to elude the Philadores, yet the truth remained. Frankie Fuentes was a killer, and he was after her son.

Abraham hurried Kayla to the henhouse while William sat on the porch steps, looking totally uninterested in anything about the farm. From what he had seen so far, the two children seemed to be complete opposites. Kayla embraced life to the full, while William hung back and needed to be coaxed into new endeavors.

Kayla's eyes were wide with wonder as she stood on tiptoe and peered into one of the nests. She spied an egg and placed it in her basket.

"Don't the chickens get upset that their eggs are gone?" she asked.

"They will lay more tomorrow, Kayla." Abraham pointed to the corner of the henhouse. "Check there. I usually find an egg or two hidden under the hay."

The child's search proved fruitful and soon she was headed back to the house with a smile of contentment on her pretty face and a basket full of eggs.

"I'll tell Mama to make something with the eggs like Mrs. Fielding did."

"Mrs. Fielding?" Abraham asked.

"She lived in an upstairs apartment and used to take care of William and me when Mama had to work."

"I am sure she was a good woman."

"Mrs. Fielding told me she was a God-fearing woman. I wasn't sure what that meant, but I told her I didn't fear God because I loved Him."

Abraham tried not to smile, but Kayla's sincerity

touched his heart. “Hurry into the house and tell your mother that William and I are going to Mr. Raber’s farm.”

“Can I go with you?”

“Maybe next time.”

She skipped toward the house and stopped on the porch step to wave goodbye.

“Go inside, Kayla,” he called to her.

The child climbed the stairs, knocked and scooted into the house when Julia opened the door. She stood for a long moment in the doorway, staring at him. The breeze pulled at her golden hair. She caught the elusive strands and tugged them back into place before she closed the door again, leaving Abraham with a curious sensation in the pit of his stomach.

He glanced at William, who shuffled along the drive, his head down and shoulders slumped. “You act as if you would rather have stayed with your mother.”

“I would rather have stayed in Philadelphia,” the boy said with a huff. “Besides, I don’t like to get up early.”

“You are tired from your journey?”

The boy nodded. “Tired and bored.”

Abraham chuckled under his breath. With all the chores that needed to be done on the farm, William would not be bored for long.

“Grab that bucket and fill it with feed for the horses in the paddock,” Abraham said when they entered the neighbor’s barn. The bucket was heavy when filled, but William carried it to the trough and then repeated the process.

“Now we will muck the stalls.” Abraham handed the boy a pitchfork and pointed to an empty stall. “Start there.”

From the look on William’s face, Abraham knew he was not happy, but he worked hard, and if he complained, he did so under his breath.

"Next we will lay fresh straw."

William followed Abraham's lead and a bed of straw soon covered the floor of the stalls.

"You have done a good job." Abraham patted the boy's shoulder. "We will go home and do the same in my barn."

An almost imperceptible groan escaped Will's lips. Abraham pretended not to notice and led the way back to the country road that divided the two farms.

Raber's phone shack sat at the edge of the road. "Wait here, William."

Abraham opened the door and stepped into the booth. He checked the answering machine to ensure Jonathan had not called and left a message.

"Is that where the Amish keep their phones?" William asked when Abraham joined him again.

"*Yah*, Mr. Raber takes orders by phone for the furniture he makes. The *Ordnung,* the rules by which various Amish communities live, forbids phones within the home. Keeping the phone away from the house and near the property line allows Mr. Raber to stay in contact with his customers while also obeying the rule."

William pointed to the roof. "Are those solar panels?"

Abraham nodded. "They run the answering machine. You know about solar energy?"

William shrugged. "A little."

"Perhaps you will be an engineer when you get older."

The boy shook his head. "I don't think so."

"Why not?" Abraham asked.

"School's not cool."

Abraham would not ask what the boy thought was cool. From what Jonathan had said, William was drawn to the street gangs with their rap music and fast cars and even faster lifestyle. Was that what William thought was cool?

The sound of a car engine drew Abraham's attention

to the road. A souped-up sedan raced over the crest of a distant rise, going much too fast along the narrow country lane.

William stared at the car, no doubt attracted to the gaudy chrome and the heavy bass destroying the peaceful quiet.

"Hide in the phone shack." Abraham opened the door and nudged William inside.

The car approached. Abraham walked to the curb. The driver stopped and rolled down the passenger window. "I'm looking for Yoder. Made a few wrong turns, it seems. Can you give me directions?"

"You are headed the right way. The town is about four miles ahead."

"I'll need a room. Can you recommend lodging?"

"There is a hotel south of town. At the intersection of Main and High, turn left. The hotel sits about five blocks south on the left." Abraham stepped closer. "You are not from this area."

"I was in Kansas City on business and had a few days off so I decided to explore this part of the state. My hobby is writing articles for travel magazines. A story on Yoder and the Amish people might sell. If you have time, we could schedule an interview."

The last thing Abraham wanted was publicity about Yoder or his Amish neighbors. "Not much is going on around here. You might find more tourist attractions in Hutchison. They have an Amish community there."

"I'll check it out. Thanks for the information about the hotel." The man handed a business card to Abraham. "You know where to find me for the next few days in case you have time for a cup of coffee, or we could talk over lunch."

The driver waved and drove away.

Abraham made a mental note of the license plate before

he opened the door to the phone booth. His heart stopped. William stood with the phone to his ear. His eyes widened and his face flushed. He dropped the receiver onto the cradle and lowered his gaze.

"Who did you call?"

The boy shook his head. "No one."

"I will ask you once more, William. Who did you call?"

"I… I thought about calling a friend of mine from Philly."

"What is his name?"

"David."

"His full name."

"David Davila."

"Did the call connect?"

Will shook his head. "No way. There wasn't time."

"Did you call your friend from the hotel in Philadelphia?"

The boy's face reddened.

"What did you tell David?"

"Only that we were moving, but I didn't tell him where."

"Did you mention Kansas?"

"I just said we were leaving the city."

Abraham pointed the boy toward the road. "The phone is off-limits. Is that understood?"

"Yeah, sure." William pushed past Abraham.

Abraham glanced back at the phone. William was his own worst enemy. The Philadores did not care if the boy was fourteen or forty-three. He was on their hit list. If Abraham could not protect William from himself, the boy and his sweet sister and pretty mother might die.

THREE

Julia felt a swell of relief when she spied William and Abraham return to the farm and enter the barn.

A short time later, the clip-clop of horses' hooves pulled her attention back to the road. A buggy turned into the drive and stopped near the barn. A woman dressed in the typical Amish calf-length blue dress, black cape and matching black bonnet climbed to the ground.

Abraham stepped from the barn and greeted her with a welcoming smile. Julia wished she could hear their conversation and wondered what she should do if the woman came inside. Was she supposed to hide?

William stood at the barn entrance. From the way his arms moved, Abraham appeared to be introducing her son to the woman. Taking that as a sign she could go outside, Julia called for Kayla to join her and they both stepped onto the porch.

Abraham glanced up and nodded. "Sarah, this is Julia. She will be staying in the *dawdy* house for a bit of time and helping with the cleaning and cooking. Her daughter's name is Kayla."

Sarah looked perplexed, but she covered her confusion with a weak smile of welcome. "Abraham said you needed a place to stay."

How should she answer? "He has been most generous to us."

"I... I brought clothing."

The Amish woman glanced at Abraham, said something that sounded German and then reached into the buggy and pulled forth a basket. "Perhaps I should show you how to pin the dress?"

Julia didn't understand.

Abraham must have noticed her confusion. He stepped closer. "I saw Sarah yesterday before you arrived and asked her to bring Amish clothing, which will be good for you to wear."

"You want me to dress Amish?"

He nodded. "For now. So you can fit in."

"And the children?"

"They should, also."

Julia glanced at Kayla who clapped her hands and jumped up and down. William frowned and wrapped his arms across his chest.

Seemed there were complications to their new environment. Julia tried to recall if the marshals had said they would be living *with* the Amish or living Amish.

A huge difference, which she would need to explain to her children. Would William listen? From the scowl on his face, probably not.

Abraham poured another cup of coffee and waited in the kitchen as Sarah ushered Julia and Kayla into a spare bedroom and helped them dress. William headed for a small room off the main living area.

"You would like help?" Abraham asked.

The boy shook his head. "I've got it."

But evidently he did not *have it* because he remained in the room far longer than Abraham had expected. Before he could check on the boy, the bedroom door opened and Kayla skipped into the kitchen. Seeing Abraham, she stopped short.

Her cheeks were flushed, and her eyes twinkled as she smiled shyly. "Sarah said she has a daughter who used to wear this dress. Now she's grown taller. Sarah said I look like an Amish girl."

Abraham had to smile. "You look very pretty, Kayla, and very Amish." Her hair was braided and pulled into a bun. "We must get you a white *kapp* in town."

"Sarah said girls cover their heads when they pray and since they always pray, they always wear their hats."

"Called a *kapp*," he instructed.

"William wears baseball caps sometimes."

"That is not the same thing."

The girl nodded. "Sarah's fixing Mama's hair so she can look Amish, too."

Footsteps sounded. Abraham looked up to see Julia standing in the hallway, eyes downcast and a troubled frown on her oval face. She wore the typical Amish blue dress with white apron tied around her slender waist. Any self-sufficiency he had noticed earlier in her demeanor had been replaced with an alluring femininity that caused his gut to tighten. He also noted a hint of confusion that creased her brow, as if leaving her ordinary world and stepping into the Amish realm had thrown her off-kilter. Perhaps dressing Amish was too much too soon. The woman had been through so much.

Sarah encouraged her forward. "Trotter's Dry Goods sells *kapps*. You must go to town and buy one for Kayla and Julia. Another dress, too, and a second apron."

He nodded. "We will go soon."

"I could meet you there and help with the selection."

"If we need help, I will let you know."

Sarah nodded and glanced at Kayla. "Tell me which you like best, apple pie or sweet potato?"

"Apple," Kayla said.

"I have an extra pie in the wagon."

Abraham smiled. "Thank you, Sarah."

"It is the least I can do." She turned and grabbed Julia's hand. "I do not know the reason you are here, but I know it must be important. Embracing the Amish life is not easy. Should you need another woman with whom to talk, tell Abraham you would like to visit. Perhaps one day this week. I will be finishing one of my quilts and could use help."

"I'm not sure you would approve of my stitches."

"We all must learn, *yah*?"

Julia smiled. "I hope someday to find a way to repay you."

"Payment is not necessary. We are neighbors and now friends. My help is freely given."

Sarah stepped toward Abraham and took his hand. "It is always good to see you, Abraham."

"Thank you, Sarah."

"You will come for dinner on Sunday?" she asked. "The bishop and his wife will be at my house."

"Not this week. Perhaps some other time."

She stepped closer and smiled knowingly. "Someday you will be ready, *yah*?"

Then she hurried around him and patted Kayla's shoulder. "Come with me, child. You can bring the pie into the house."

Abraham watched her climb into the buggy and hand a pie to Kayla. The girl hurried back inside.

"Place the pie on the counter," Abraham instructed. "We will have a slice after we eat this evening."

Kayla returned to the porch and waved goodbye to Sarah. Julia stood near the sink as if glued in place.

"I am sure wearing an Amish dress is not what you expected." Abraham tried to explain. "Jonathan felt the disguise would add another layer of protection."

"He's right. It's just a change." She offered him a weak smile, and then, with a sigh, stepped closer to the sink and washed a glass left on the counter. "Sarah seems like a nice woman."

"She goes out of her way to be helpful." Abraham took another sip of coffee.

"You are courting, perhaps?"

He furrowed his brow. "Did she say this?"

"No, of course not. It's just she mentioned her husband had died." Julia reached for the towel and dried her hands. "I saw Sarah's expression when she looked at you. I thought—"

"You thought wrong." For whatever reason, Julia's comment irritated him. "William is still in the small room at the front of the house, probably refusing to change clothes. You best check on him."

Abraham grabbed his hat from the wall peg and stomped outside. His anger changed to concern when he spotted William heading into the barn from the driveway, still wearing his *Englisch* clothing. Abraham glanced back at his house and then at the phone shack in the distance. The door he had closed earlier now hung open.

His heart stopped. The boy had left Abraham's house through the front door and had returned to the phone booth, probably to call his friend. If William had shared his whereabouts with David, the information could easily spread throughout the Philadelphia neighborhood and eventually to the Philadores. Within a day or two at the most, the gang would descend on Yoder, Kansas, in search of a fourteen-year-old boy who, in their opinion, needed to be offed.

Abraham would talk to William, but first he had to alert Jonathan. He hurried to the phone shack, stepped inside and hit the button that would reveal the last number called. He jotted down the sequence of digits on a piece of scratch paper and tapped in Jonathan's number.

"We have a problem," Abraham said in greeting. He quickly relayed what had happened and provided the phone number William had contacted. "Have Karl pick up the family and find another safe place for them to hide out."

"No can do, Abe, at least not now. Fuentes is beating the bushes, trying to find Will. Moving the family would be too dangerous. They have to stay with you until things calm down."

"You are taking too big of a risk, Jonathan."

"I'm keying the phone number William called into my computer. Give me a minute or two and we'll see what I can find."

"Find a new hiding place for Julia and her children. If the gang learns their whereabouts, they will be sitting ducks, as the saying goes."

"Hopefully the kid in Philly will keep his mouth shut."

Abraham let out a frustrated breath. "The kid's name is David Davila. If you count on him keeping silent, you are toying with William's life."

"We'll work as fast as we can, Abe, but nothing is done in the blink of an eye. You know that."

"I know when someone is in danger and needs protection."

"That's why I placed them with you."

"While you are checking, run the name Nelson Turner.

He asked for directions to Yoder. Said he was a writer." Abraham provided the license plate number for the sports car.

"Writer or journalist? I'll check the plates, but my advice is to stay clear of anyone involved with the media. The last thing we want is Julia or her children's photo in the paper or on some online news blog."

"That was my thought, as well."

Jonathan clucked his tongue. "I found the address associated with the phone number William called. Now I'll cross-check it with known gang members in the area."

A sigh filled the line.

Abraham pushed the receiver closer to his ear. "What?"

"William's friend, David, lives at the same address as a low-level punk who we think has ties to the Philadores. Pablo… Pablo Davila. They must be brothers."

"David is probably filling his brother in on William's whereabouts as we speak."

"Point taken. I'll pull some strings and see if we can speed up the process of creating new identities for the family. But remember, Abraham, Kansas is a big state. Fuentes is looking for a woman and kids wearing jeans and sweaters. Keep them dressed Amish for their own safety. As we both know, Fuentes is a killer. The last thing we want is for Julia and her son William to be injured or end up dead."

Dead, like Marianne and Becca. Abraham's stomach soured. "Move mountains, Jonathan, and get this family to a more secure location."

"We'll work this end, Abe, but I'm relying on you to keep them safe until then."

Safe and alive. Was Jonathan counting too heavily on Abraham? He had not been able to protect his own family. Would he be able to protect Julia and her children?

FOUR

Julia had watched her son scurry into the barn. Abraham had then raced across the country road to the neighbor's farm. When she stretched on tiptoe, she could see to the end of the neighbor's driveway where the small guardhouse-like building stood near the two-lane road.

At first glance, she'd thought it an outhouse, but realizing the location was much too public for the modest Amish, she ran off a checklist of what could be contained within the shelter and came up empty. What she did realize was that something was wrong when Abraham bounded back across the road and followed the path her son had taken into the barn. Her stomach tightened as concern swept over her.

She could tell Abraham was upset from the way he held himself, tense, unsettled and she feared angry, as well.

She glanced down at the Amish clothing she was wearing and wondered yet again at the circumstances that had led her to Kansas. At least she and her children had eluded the Philadores and had escaped from the inner city. Yet, at the present moment, she questioned their security here on this Amish farm. If their generous host was upset with William, he could easily call Jonathan and ask that they be moved to another location.

She let out a lungful of pent-up air, conjuring up memories of their five days in the hotel and the uncertainty of not knowing where they would be placed. As much as she appreciated the marshals' desire to keep them safe, she did not want to face that uncertainty again.

She glanced at the table where Kayla was pretending to feed her doll baby with wood chips she had collected from the box near the stove.

"Stay inside with Marianne while I see what William is doing in the barn."

"Her name is Annie."

"What?" Julia stepped closer. "Who's Annie?"

"My doll. Abraham said he would call her Annie so I'm calling her Annie, too. It's her Amish name. Plus, she's in witness protection so she needed a new name."

"You aren't to mention WitSec, Kayla."

"I won't say anything to anyone except you and William and Mr. Abraham. And Marshal Preston and Marshal Adams and Marshal Mast, too. Will we see them again, Mama?"

"I'm sure we will, but right now, I need to talk to William. You and Annie stay inside. I'll be in the barn."

"Did William do something wrong?"

"Why do you ask?"

"Because he's acting like he's not happy here. I told him living on a farm is better than in the city."

"What was William's reply?"

Kayla shook her head. "He didn't say anything. He's pretending he doesn't want to talk to me 'cause he had to leave his friends. Only they weren't really his friends."

"Why do you say that?"

"They weren't nice to me."

Concerned, Julia threaded her fingers through her

daughter's blond hair. "Did something happen while I was at work? Something you didn't tell me?"

"No, Mama. It's just that David wanted Will to sneak out of Ms. Fielding's apartment. But I told him he had to stay inside so you didn't have to worry."

At least one of her children had a good head on her shoulders. Kayla was wise beyond her years.

"Your brother will get his life straightened out one of these days, Kayla."

"I hope so."

Julia hoped so, too.

She opened the kitchen door and hurried to the barn. Her stomach roiled as she thought of what might be transpiring between their Amish host and her son. Worried, she stepped into the darkened interior and narrowed her gaze, hoping to see William before he saw her.

He stood in one of the stalls, holding a pitchfork in his hands and staring up at Abraham.

"You were not thinking of your mother and sister and of their safety, were you?" Abraham asked.

Will shrugged.

"When I ask you a question I expect more than a shrug."

"I dunno."

"I think you do know, William. Did you tell David you were in Kansas?"

William shook his head.

"I did not hear you."

Her son blinked. His face was pale and his eyes wide, as if he realized Abraham expected obedience even if William did not see the need to make a verbal reply.

"I am waiting for your response." Abraham's voice was firm, yet Julia heard no hint of anger, only a man who expected an honest answer.

"I...I might have mentioned Kansas," William said in a timid voice.

"Might you have mentioned the town of Yoder, and that you were staying on an Amish farm?"

"No, sir." Her son's response was immediate. If she could trust her mother's instincts, William was telling the truth.

"So your friend does not know where in Kansas, just that you and your mother and sister are living in Kansas."

"I didn't mention Kayla or my mom."

Abraham nodded. "I see. So does David think you are living alone in Kansas?"

"I don't think so."

Abraham leaned in closer. "Does David know anything about the witness protection program?"

"Maybe, but not from me. I didn't say we had a new name or that the marshals flew us here. I just said I was in Kansas."

"You called David's cell phone?"

William shook his head. "I called his house landline."

"That has Caller ID and would register the phone number you used."

"David's mom won't pay for anything extra," Will insisted. "They don't have Caller ID or Call Waiting or any other add-on."

"He could have punched in *69."

"Yes, sir, but I don't think knowing the phone number was important to Davey. I told him I'd call him back."

Abraham studied him for a long moment and then gave a quick nod of his head. "Is there anything else you think I should know?"

"Only that the Philadores are looking for me."

Julia's heart broke, seeing the downward cast of William's eyes and the pull at his mouth. When was the last time her son had been a happy, carefree boy? Would he ever be one again?

"That is why you are here, William. You understand that, do you not? You are here so the Philadores cannot find you. That is why we do not want them to have any phone numbers they could trace."

"Even if Davey knew the phone number, he wouldn't give it to his brother or to any of the gang members."

Abraham's shoulders sagged with frustration, as if, at that moment, he realized William truly did not comprehend the danger he was in.

No one should feel hunted or preyed upon. Especially not a fourteen-year-old boy who did not understand the full meaning of gang warfare and retaliation.

"No more phone calls, William. Is that understood?"

"Yes, sir. I understand."

"*Gut.*" Abraham hesitated a moment before adding, "I expect you to wear Amish clothing. After you finish mucking the stall, go inside and change your clothes."

He turned and walked toward the open barn door with determined steps, nearly bumping into Julia who hovered in the shadows just inside the entrance.

She put her finger to his lips, motioned him outside and stopped when they were halfway to the house. "I overheard you talking to William. Did he call David?"

"He did." Abraham pointed to the shack at the edge of his neighbor's property. "On Harvey Raber's phone."

"You're pointing to the little house by the road?" she asked.

Abraham nodded. "The phone shack. Harvey uses the phone for business and emergency needs. He allows his neighbors to make calls, too."

"I apologize for William's actions. He has changed over the last year or so. Age has a lot to do with it, but so does where we lived. Now the people he wanted to associate with in the city are after him."

"Yet he does not understand the danger, Julia."

Which was exactly what she had been thinking.

"It is the problem with youth," Abraham continued. "Especially *Englisch* youth. They live in the moment and act irrationally. Someone hurts a kid on the street and they strike back, then they get their friends to strike back. That only escalates the unrest and violence."

"And mushrooms into gang warfare in the inner city." She knew it all too well.

"I saw it when I was a cop. Boys grow up without fathers and without good role models who provide sound advice and guidance. Children—most especially boys—need a strong male presence in their lives so they can understand what it means to be a man."

"I agree, but some fathers are not good role models. William's father is in jail. That's hard for a kid to overcome."

Abraham nodded. "Yet I can see that you have tried to be what he was not. William is at a difficult time of life and questioning everything. I did the same at his age."

"I'm sure you weren't attracted to gangs and violence."

"Only because I had a faith that served as a moral compass. Plus, the people I knew—my father and uncles and other leaders in my community—were strong men. I wanted to work for good and not evil and knew this, even though I longed to experience life outside the Amish community."

"What made you want to leave?"

He shrugged. "I was looking at the world through teenage eyes and did not see the big picture, as the saying goes. A young Amish boy had been kidnapped. The parents listened to the bishop who did not believe the *Englisch* authorities needed to be notified."

"And the child?"

"Was never found. Growing up, I always wondered what would have happened if law enforcement had been called in to investigate. I wanted to be the man who saved that little boy."

Julia touched his arm. "Jonathan told me about your wife and daughter. I'm sorry."

"Sometimes Jonathan talks too much."

He started to walk away, but she tugged on his arm. "Don't be upset. Jonathan knew I would understand a portion of your pain. He said a paroled criminal came after you and killed your family. That's my fear. I can never stop thinking about William, knowing he could end up dead. Kayla, too. I don't know how you survived."

"The truth is that I wanted to die, but God did not grant me that desire. Instead He sent Jonathan to help me heal."

"Perhaps God knew my children and I would need you."

Abraham tilted his head, as if pondering what she had said, and stared down at her for a long moment. The intensity of his gaze filled her with sorrow at the depth of pain he carried.

Then, with a jerk of his head, he glanced back at the barn. "William will finish cleaning one of the stalls soon. I noticed the schoolbooks you brought from Philadelphia. If you have work for him to do, it must wait until after we go to town. The sole on one of his shoes has ripped apart. He needs work boots to protect his feet."

"Town?"

"Yoder. It is not far. Kayla needs new shoes, and so do you."

Julia glanced down at her flats. "I have shoes."

"Those will not last long on a farm. As Sarah mentioned, you and Kayla also need *kapps*."

"Are you sure?"

"*Yah*, I am sure. When we come home, I will prepare the evening meal and will ring the dinner bell at six o'clock. This will give you enough time for the schoolwork."

"It will. Thank you. Tomorrow I will cook."

"We will wait until tomorrow to decide on the day's meals. A lot can happen in the next few hours."

He turned and walked to the paddock, leaving her to ponder his words, which hopefully were not prophetic. William and Kayla were safe on this Amish farm, at least for now.

She could breathe easy, although Julia was still concerned about her children's well-being. The Philadores were a vile gang that would stop at nothing to get her son.

Keep William safe, she prayed, knowing God wouldn't be listening. He had other people He loved more and who were more important to Him.

Julia was a woman who had made too many mistakes. Her own father had called her a mistake, and she'd never been able to shed the label.

She had a lot to learn about faith and putting her trust in God. She watched as Abraham harnessed one of the horses. She needed to trust God and Abraham. If only she could.

Kayla tugged at Abraham's heart. Her blue eyes and sweet smile brought back memories of Becca. His daughter had been only four years old, but she had wrapped Abraham around her little finger. Like his daughter, Kayla was bubbly and energetic, and the opposite of William, who slumped into periods of moodiness. The boy needed to learn the benefits of hard work. He would forget about what he had left behind when he started to feel proud of what he was able to accomplish on the farm.

"Sit next to your sister," Abraham instructed as the boy climbed into the buggy dressed in the Amish shirt and trousers Sarah had gotten from a neighbor. "You need a hat, William."

"A *kapp*?"

"*Kapps* are for the ladies. You need a felt hat. Once warm weather arrives, the men switch from felt to straw hats."

"I don't want a hat."

"*Yah*?"

The boy nodded. "*Yah*."

William's tone was emphatic and sarcastic. Abraham ignored the disrespect. A headstrong horse was hard to break. A boy could be the same. Abraham would be patient and consistent in both discipline and praise.

He glanced at the *dawdy* house. What was keeping Julia?

The door opened and she stepped onto the porch. As she neared, he noticed a hint of excitement in her eyes. Unlike the boy, Julia and her daughter seemed more eager to embrace the Amish way.

He took her hand and helped her into the buggy.

"Sit in front next to me," he suggested.

"Thank you." She lowered her gaze and adjusted her skirt. "I've never ridden in a buggy before."

"You will find it enjoyable, I hope."

"What's the horse's name?" Kayla asked from the rear.

"Buttercup."

"Mama said my daddy called me Butterbean."

Julia sighed ever so slightly.

"Your father loved you, I am sure," Abraham said,

hoping to assuage the child's need for acceptance and affirmation.

"Sometimes I have trouble remembering him." Her tone was grown-up and matter-of-fact, yet she was never without the doll her father had given her clasped tightly in her arms.

Abraham glanced at Julia. From the struggle he saw in her eyes, he wondered again about the husband. Both Jonathan and Julia had mentioned he was serving time. Hard for kids to know their father was in jail.

"What should we expect in town?" Julia asked as Abraham flicked the reins and turned the mare onto the main road. Buttercup's hooves pounded over the pavement.

"Remember your new last name in Stolz," he said. "I do not think people will ask, but you are my sister Susan's friend. She knew I needed help with my house."

"Why do we have to make up a story?" Kayla asked.

"Because the Philadores want to hurt me," William mumbled.

"You never should have gone outside the night of the street fight."

"Be quiet, Kayla."

"Children!" Julia turned, her finger raised. "We will not say anything unless it is something positive about the other. Is that understood?"

"Yes, Mama," Kayla replied.

"Whatever," William groaned.

Julia turned back to the road. "What if people ask me about being Amish?"

"You can say you are deciding whether to join the faith."

"I don't speak German, Abraham. You said a few things to Sarah I couldn't understand."

"The dialect is Pennsylvania Dutch. You will be fine

speaking English. Just say you are studying to become Amish if anyone quizzes you."

"William doesn't like quizzes," Kayla tattled.

"I do, too."

"Not when you don't know the answers."

Julia raised her hand again. The children quieted.

"I'm sorry, Abraham, about their outbursts."

He smiled. "My sister and I were the same."

"I've heard the Amish practice shunning when they leave the faith. Is that what happened to you?"

"I was not baptized, so I was not actually shunned. Although my *datt*, my father, refused to speak to me after I left home."

"I'm sure he was overjoyed when you returned to your faith."

"He died the year before I returned to be baptized."

"I'm sorry."

So was Abraham. He glanced back to ensure the road behind them was clear. "We'll stop at a store on the outskirts of town."

"The one Sarah mentioned?"

"*Yah*. It is just ahead."

He guided Buttercup around a bend in the road and into the store's parking area. After tethering the horse to the hitching rail, he lifted Kayla from the buggy. Julia climbed down after William. Her foot slipped. Abraham wrapped his arms around her waist and guided her to the ground.

"You must be careful," he cautioned.

"I tripped on my skirt. Jeans would be less of a problem."

"You are right." He motioned them toward the door.

The clerk, a young Amish woman, approached as they entered. "May I help you find something?"

"I need a *kapp*." Julia pointed to Kayla. "And so does my daughter."

"What size do you wear?"

Julia looked quizzically at Abraham who shrugged.

"I came from another area," Julia said, covering her confusion. "Our sizes were different. Not too small. Not too large."

"You can see them in the back. There is a mirror." The clerk pointed Julia to the small dressing room. Kayla skipped behind them.

"We must find a hat for you." Abraham put his hand on William's slender shoulder. The boy balked, but Abraham ushered him toward the far side of the store where the men's hats hung on the wall.

The scowl on William's face lifted after he checked the price tag on one of the hats. Money talked in the gang world, and whether the boy equated the expensive hat with status in the Amish world, Abraham would never know, but William's negative attitude softened somewhat.

After trying on a number of wide-brimmed, felt hats, they decided on one that fit. "It suits you well," Abraham said once they made the selection.

The door to the dressing room opened and Kayla came out smiling. The white starched *kapp* covered her bun. "*Mamm* says I look lovely."

"*Mamm*?" Kayla had used the Amish word for mom or mama.

"*Yah*." She dipped her head and smiled, as if proud of the newly acquired word she had evidently picked up from the clerk.

"There is a flea market in town next week," the woman said to Julia as they joined Abraham and William. "It is a nice day for families."

The clerk glanced at Abraham. "You are going, perhaps?"

"Perhaps. How much do I owe you?" He paid with cash and hurried Julia and the children outside.

A siren sounded and lights flashed. The sheriff had pulled a red sports car to the side of the road. A tall, slender teen with tattoos and piercings glanced at them. His gaze lingered on Julia. A second, equally tatted kid stared through the passenger window.

A buggy, driven by an older Amish man, turned into the lot and parked next to Abraham's rig. "Trouble has come to Yoder," the elderly man grumbled.

"What happened?" Abraham asked.

"The driver was speeding through town, but the sheriff will set him straight, *yah*? Samuel Hershberger's buggy was run off the road last week when a red sports car cut him off. My guess it is the same car. Why do the *Englisch* not let us live in peace?"

Abraham had often wondered the same thing.

He helped Julia into the buggy.

"We should go home," she said, her face tight with worry.

"After we buy shoes."

As the buggy passed the stopped car, Abraham made a mental note of the license plate.

"Did you see an *P* monogramed on the baseball hat the guy in the car was wearing?" Julia bit her lip and glanced back, her eyes wide. "He could have been a Philador. They sometimes tattoo an *P* on their hands."

"The car has a Kansas plate, Julia. They are local punks. Do not worry."

Philadelphia was over a thousand miles away, and the Philadores had yet to set up a presence in this part of the country. Still, Fuentes could have expanded his reach.

While Abraham wanted to soothe Julia's concerns, he would keep watch for the sports car and the two teens. Better safe than sorry, especially when a woman and her two children were in danger.

FIVE

Julia wanted to go back to the farm. The men who'd been stopped by the sheriff had unsettled her. Plus, she didn't want to pretend to be Amish and have to fend off questions like the ones the clerk at the store had asked about where she was from and how she knew Abraham. She hoped her responses had been general enough to not raise the clerk's suspicions.

But she worried about the next person who questioned her. Surely she would say something wrong that would give away their identities. If she didn't, her children would.

How could the marshals think this was a good way to keep them safe? Instead of feeling protected, Julia felt exposed and vulnerable.

"The shoes can wait until another day," she said to Abraham.

"We are already in town. There is no reason to turn back now."

Once again, she glanced around the side of the buggy and stared at the flashing lights on the sheriff's sedan. "Does the sheriff know you work for the marshals?"

"I do not work for them, Julia. Jonathan is a friend who asked if I could help. No one here knows about either of us being involved with witness protection, so it is not something we should discuss."

"I wasn't discussing it, I was merely asking a question." Frustration bubbled up. Did Abraham not realize how dangerous it was to be riding through town in a buggy? Surely everyone would stare at them.

But when Julia looked at the people milling around on the street, they seemed oblivious to her and her children. Perhaps because many of the other people were dressed in Amish clothing, and everywhere she looked, she saw buggies. Some driven by women, most driven by men. Children sat perched in the rear and stared at the passing cars.

The scene was as foreign to her as living in the inner city had been when she and the children had first moved there. Maybe more so.

She wrung her hands and tried to calm her unease by reading the signs that hung above the shops—The Tack Shop, Eicher's Feed, *Yoder Gazette*.

Abraham seemed oblivious to her concerns.

"Where's the shoe store?" she finally asked.

"On the next block."

She stretched to see into the distance. "I only see a hardware store and restaurant."

"The hardware store sells shoes, Julia."

"Only in Yoder, right?"

He looked at her and smiled. "You will get used to the local ways."

Abraham parked the buggy in the rear of the store and pointed them through a side door. The expansive interior was paneled in knotty pine and lit with bright fluorescent lighting.

The clerk nodded a greeting. "Morning, Abraham."

"Silas." Abraham motioned the children and Julia forward. "We are in need of shoes for these children and their mother."

"I will measure their feet."

Once the measurements were taken, Silas brought out boxes of shoes. William's eyes brightened when he spied a pair of work books. "They look like Doc Martens."

"Only they will hold up better," the clerk assured him.

Kayla tried on a pair of leather shoes with laces. "They fit, *Mamm*."

Julia leaned closer. "Did your last shoes not fit?"

"They pinched my toes, but I didn't want to tell you."

Seven years old, yet sensitive beyond her age.

"My feet are happy in these shoes," Kayla said with a wide smile. "I'll be able to run and skip and jump again."

Julia's heart hurt. Tears burned her eyes. What kind of mother was she not to have realized her daughter needed new shoes? Money had been tight, but she would have cut back on something else. If there had been anything else to cut back on.

Abraham was staring at her.

She averted her gaze, feeling foolish and emotional. Plus, she was still so tired.

He stepped closer. "You need shoes. Something sturdy."

She looked down at her flats. The aches in her legs were, no doubt, from wearing shoes without support and too many hours on her feet working in the diner while Mrs. Fielding watched the children.

"What do Amish women usually wear?" Julia asked.

He held up a pair of black leather lace-up shoes.

"They're not very fashionable."

He laughed. "The farm is not a place for fashion."

"You're probably right."

She tried on the shoes and was surprised at how the soft leather cushioned her feet. Now she understood what Kayla was saying about her feet feeling happy.

"May I wear them home?" she asked.

"*Yah.*" Abraham paid for the shoes. "Now we will get ice cream for an afternoon treat."

Kayla's eyes widened. "Mr. Abraham, that sounds *gut.*"

He chuckled. "You are quite the linguist, Kayla."

"*Mamm* says I'm smart."

"Your mother is right."

He smiled at Julia, and for a moment she felt the weight lift from her shoulders. Then she thought again of the gang that was after her son.

Her pulse raced as she glanced around the store. "Where's William?"

Abraham's face drained of color. He turned to look. "Stay here."

But she couldn't. Not when her son was missing.

She grabbed Kayla's hand and followed Abraham out of the store. Her heart pounded a warning when she thought of the men in the sports car.

"Where's William?" Kayla asked.

"I don't know, honey."

Why had she let him out of her sight?

Abraham hurried around the corner and headed to the rear of the building.

"*Please!*" Julia lifted up a partial prayer to a God who never listened.

She turned the corner with Kayla in tow and stopped short, seeing Abraham a few feet ahead. He was staring at the buggy where William stood, raking his fingers through Buttercup's mane.

Stepping closer to Abraham, she sighed. "My heart stopped beating about two minutes ago."

"I should have looked here first. He loves the animals."

"I...I thought something had happened to him."

"We could not find you, William," Abraham said when

the boy looked up and noticed them. "Next time, you must tell your mother where you are going."

"I don't have to ask her permission."

"A child does not disrespect a parent." Abraham's voice was firm. He pointed to the buggy. "Get in."

The boy huffed and climbed all the way into the rear.

Abraham hefted Kayla onto the second seat.

"What about getting ice cream, Mr. Abraham?"

"Not today, Kayla."

William slumped in the back of the buggy, his eyes downcast, looking sullen and unresponsive. A look Julia knew too well.

Julia climbed in beside her daughter. She didn't want to sit next to Abraham. Not when her son had caused them such a scare and had been so disrespectful.

She wrapped her arm around Kayla and pulled her close.

Abraham flipped the reins and turned the buggy onto the main road. Buttercup began to trot as they left town.

Clouds covered the once-bright sun and warned of an encroaching storm. Everything had gone from bad to worse in the blink of an eye.

After what William had done today, Julia was sure Abraham would insist they leave, but if he forced them away, where would they go?

SIX

Julia had trouble falling asleep that night. She kept hearing footsteps and imagining her son had left the house and was now in the middle of a street fight just as had happened in Philadelphia.

She got up twice and each time stared out the window, seeing the main house and the still countryside. Surely she and her family were safe here in Kansas, yet the Philadores were looking for her son. A heaviness settled on her shoulders as she thought of William's phone call to David and how easily one slip of the tongue could have revealed their whereabouts. How had life gotten so complicated?

Returning to bed, she pounded her fist into her pillow and flipped onto her side, facing away from the window and the first light of dawn that peeked around the edge of the curtain.

She dozed for all too short a time and then jerked awake, still fearful for William's well-being. After pulling herself from bed, she slipped on her robe and stepped into the hallway where she glanced at Kayla, sleeping peacefully in the room across the hallway. The doll Charlie had given her was still clutched in her arms.

Julia shook her head at the sad irony of a child who clung to a doll as a substitute for the love she longed to receive from her father.

She continued along the hall and stopped on the threshold of William's room, noting how high his bedding was piled. She moved quietly into the room and lifted the edge of the quilt, expecting to see William. Instead of her son, she found two pillows waded into a ball.

Her heart stopped.

She threw the quilt off the bed, then turned and ran down the steps. Fighting back tears, she checked the remaining rooms before she returned to the kitchen. She pulled open the door and raced across the yard to the main house.

"Abraham, wake up." She pounded on his door. "Abraham."

The door flew open. His hair was tousled, his face puffy with sleep. "What is wrong?"

"William." Tears filled her eyes. "He's gone."

Adrenaline had kicked in as soon as Abraham heard the insistent knocking on the door. Seeing Julia, her eyes wide with fear, her mouth drawn and her face pale, sent a jolt of panic to wrap around his heart.

"Did you search the house?" he asked.

"I did."

She glanced back at the *dawdy* house. "I heard something a few hours ago that sounded like footsteps, only I talked myself into believing it was just the house creaking." She put her hand to her mouth. "Oh, Abraham, how could I have been so foolish?"

"I will search the grounds. Change into street clothes, then wake Kayla and get her dressed. She can wear her Amish dress, if she wants. We will ask Sarah to watch her while we look for William."

Grabbing a flashlight, Abraham raced to the barn and outbuildings, calling William's name. From there, he crossed the road and entered his neighbor's barn. He checked the stalls to make certain the boy was not hiding in one of the dark corners and then ran to the phone shack.

The answering machine blinked.

He entered the code and listened as a male voice left a message. "William, this is David. Look, I can't get to Kansas City in time, but my brother Pablo will be there. He'll meet your bus. You can fly with him back to Philly. Pablo said he'll keep you safe."

Either William had lied or somehow David had gotten Harvey Raber's phone number. Abraham made a fist and wanted to smash his hand through the wall. Instead, he reached for the phone and tapped in the number for the Amish taxi, grateful that the taxi driver prided himself on being available around the clock.

"Randy, this is Abraham King. I need your services. Come as quickly as possible."

The taxi pulled into the driveway not more than twenty minutes later. Abraham forsook his waistcoat and grabbed a black hooded sweatshirt from his room and slipped it on as he hurried to the *dawdy* house.

Julia opened the door before he knocked. She was dressed in jeans and a sweater with a lightweight jacket. "Did you find him?"

He shook his head and explained about David's message on the answering machine.

A faint gasp escaped Julia's lips, then she turned to where Kayla sat at the table, rubbing her eyes, and motioned the child forward. Her hair was pulled into a makeshift bun. She wore her Amish dress and carried her *kapp* in one hand and her doll in the other.

"You called a cab?" Julia asked, seeing the car in the drive.

"An Amish cab. Randy is a good driver. We will go

first to Sarah's house. Kayla can stay there while we look for William."

Julia nodded and ushered Kayla into the car. Randy seemed to understand that speed was of the essence. He turned the car radio to an easy listening channel, which would ensure Abraham and Julia could talk without being overheard. Instead of conversing, both of them seemed lost in their own thoughts and were silent as Randy pulled the taxi onto the main road and drove quickly to Sarah's farm.

Abraham was the first to alight from the car once it stopped in front of the farmhouse. Julia and Kayla followed close behind him. He knocked on the door, hoping Sarah was in the kitchen preparing breakfast.

She peered through the window before opening the door. "What's wrong?"

"William left the house sometime in the night. We need to find him. He may have taken a bus to another city. Can you watch Kayla while we are gone?"

"*Yah*, of course." Sarah reached out to Julia and squeezed her hand. "Do not worry. Kayla will be fine with us."

"Thank you, Sarah."

Julia hugged her daughter. "We'll be back as soon as possible. Mind Miss Sarah."

"I will, Mama."

As soon as the door closed, Julia hurried back to the car. Abraham climbed in next to her. "The bus station in town, Randy. As fast as you can."

Julia dropped her head into her hands. "I'm so worried."

"We will find him." Abraham wanted to reassure her, but he was worried, as well.

"Why would David leave a message on your neighbor's phone?" she asked.

"He probably thought William had access to the voice mail. The boys cooked up this rendezvous in Kansas City, never realizing the implications." Or the danger to William, he failed to add. Thankfully, the outgoing message on Harvey's answering machine was generic and did not mention his business or its location.

"David's brother is working with the Philadores," Julia said, her voice low. "I saw him a few times and knew his mother. She's a nice woman, struggling to keep her kids safe. William didn't have much to do with Pablo, which doesn't bode well for the two of them meeting up in Kansas City." She shook her head. "How does William plan to get there?"

"I keep the motor coach schedule on the bookshelf in the main room. William must have seen it yesterday before he called David. A bus left the Yoder station at six this morning, heading first to Topeka and then on to Kansas City."

"He doesn't have money to buy a ticket."

"Check your wallet."

She opened her purse and pulled out her wallet. Her face dropped. "He took money from my purse."

Julia shook her head. "I never thought my son would steal from me."

"He probably plans to pay you back, although I am not sure how he will earn the money. But then, kids do not think things through."

"Oh, Abraham. What am I to do?"

"We'll check at the bus station. Surely the clerk will remember if a young boy bought a ticket. If he did not, then we will search through Yoder and the surrounding area."

"And if he bought a ticket?" she asked, her eyes filled with worry.

"Then we will go to Kansas City."

"What if Pablo is waiting there for him?"

"We will face that when it happens. Right now, we need to determine if William was on that bus." Abraham reached for her hand. "We will find him, Julia."

"I was too hard on him."

He shook his head. "The boy needs to understand what is expected. This is not your fault."

"He's a child."

"At fourteen, he is almost a man. An Amish youth would be plowing fields, driving wagons and taking care of livestock. You underestimate your son."

"He didn't grow up on a farm. He grew up in a middle class neighborhood outside of Philadelphia, until his father gambled away everything we had."

She raked her hand through her hair. "Charlie didn't want children. He said I never gave him any time after William was born. He didn't realize what parenting involved and thought only of what he wanted."

"What happened after you had Kayla?"

"That's the irony," she said with a sigh. "He adored his daughter while ignoring William. He knew his father didn't love him. He didn't hold that against Kayla, but he held it against Charlie."

"Your husband left you soon after Kayla was born?"

"Not until she was in preschool. I kicked him out. He was taking all the money he earned along with whatever he could find from my paycheck. He gave me no choice."

She turned to look out the window and lowered her voice. "Plus he became abusive."

"What?"

She held up her hand. "Not physically, although he

threatened me. That's when we moved. I didn't think he could find me, but he sent a package to the new house. It was a present for Kayla. She opened it before I realized what she was doing and found the doll she now calls Annie."

Julia tugged at a strand of hair and glanced at Randy, who was oblivious to their discussion.

"William looked into the box," she continued. "I knew he was searching for a gift for himself, but there was nothing. We moved again, this time into the city. I didn't want Charlie to know where we were. Not long after that, I saw in the paper that he had been arrested for embezzling money from a police department fund for officers who had been wounded or killed in the line of duty."

"He was found guilty?"

She nodded. "And sent to prison. Soon after that, William started talking about various gang members and what the Philadores were doing in the neighborhood. He only saw what he wanted to see. He didn't realize how they intimidated people and shoved their weight around. That's when I took both children out of school and taught them at home. A sweet neighbor watched them while I worked at night. I kept my thumb on William, only he still slipped away from me at times, which is what he's done again."

Abraham glanced out the window. "The bus station is on the corner of the next block. You stay with Randy while I check inside."

"I want to go with you."

As the taxi pulled to a stop, Julia stared through the car window. "How did William find his way here?"

"Probably from the bus brochure. A map on the back of the brochure shows where the station is located. The Amish rely on buses to visit relatives and friends in neighboring towns, and the buses run frequently."

"He can't be gone, Abraham. I can't lose him."

But when they entered the station and saw only a few Amish people waiting for the next bus, Abraham had a sick feeling in the pit of his stomach. He headed for the clerk.

"We are looking for a young boy, age fourteen, who may have bought a ticket to Kansas City in the last few hours."

The clerk nodded. "Brown hair, wearing a Philadelphia Eagles sweatshirt?"

"William loves that sweatshirt. You saw him?" Julia glanced around the small station. "Is he still here?"

"He took the earlier bus to Topeka and then on to Kansas City, which was his destination. Is there a problem?"

"What time will that bus arrive in Kansas City?"

"With all the stops along the way, it won't get there until eleven this morning. You're looking for him, I presume? Might be able to catch up to him in Topeka."

The clerk glanced at his watch. "On second thought, I doubt you'll get there in time. If you've got a car, my suggestion would be to take the back roads to Kansas City. You should arrive just before the bus. The next motor coach heading that way leaves here in an hour, but it won't arrive in Kansas City until later this afternoon."

"Thanks for your help." Abraham grabbed Julia's hand and they hurried outside and back to the cab.

"How do we get to the city?" she asked.

Abraham peered through the open passenger window at the driver and raised his voice to be heard. "Hopefully, Randy will drive us to Kansas City."

"I haven't been to the city in almost a year, but I know the back roads," the taxi driver acknowledged with a nod. "Climb in. I'll get you there."

Abraham glanced at the sky, where dark clouds hovered on the horizon. They would be driving into a storm. But that was the least of their problems. They had to find William, and find him before Pablo Davila did.

SEVEN

Julia wanted to get behind the wheel and drive, only she would probably exceed the speed limit and crash into another vehicle, as jumpy as she felt. Why were the miles passing so slowly and the minutes so quickly?

William was on a bus heading straight into the hands of the Philadores. Maybe they should have called law enforcement, but she didn't trust cops. She glanced at Abraham who stared out the front window, his jaw tight and neck tense. He looked as worried as she felt.

She rubbed her hand over her stomach and tried to calm the nervous jitters that wreaked havoc with her composure. She wanted to cry and scream at the same time, although she continued to sit still and stare at the road, knowing if they didn't get to Kansas City in time, they wouldn't find William and her life would be over. She would have to go on because of Kayla, but losing her son would break her heart in two.

She must have groaned. Abraham turned to look at her, his eyes filled with understanding that almost crashed through the dam she had placed on her tears. She couldn't cry now. It wouldn't help anything and would make her seem weak, which she never wanted to be. Plus, it wouldn't help William. The only thing that would help him was arriving at the station before the bus.

"How much longer?" she asked, her voice little more than a whisper.

"Randy, how far are we from the city?"

The driver turned down the radio and waited until Abraham repeated the question, then he shrugged. "We're not far in miles, but you never know about traffic. Especially around midday. What time was the bus supposed to arrive?"

"Eleven."

Randy glanced at the clock. "We might make it."

"Might?" Her voice was pinched tight.

She closed her eyes, bringing to mind thoughts of when William was a little boy, thoughts of the good times instead of the bad.

Fortunately, the storm they had expected blew past, traffic moved and Randy skillfully got them to the city. They crossed over the river and onto the Missouri side.

"Which bus station?" Randy asked.

Abraham provided the address.

"We're not far from there. I'll drop you off in front. Should I hang around for a while?"

"If you can. As soon as we spot William, I will find a pay phone and call you."

"You've got my number?"

"I do."

Julia glanced at the clock on the dashboard. Eleven-fifteen. If only the bus was running behind schedule.

"Ready?" Abraham asked when the taxi pulled to the curb.

She nodded. He opened the door and stepped to the sidewalk. Julia followed, her eyes on the people exiting the bus station. She hurried through the doors with Abraham close behind her.

Both of them stopped short.

Julia's heart pounded as she searched the folks milling around the central waiting area. "I don't see him."

Abraham guided her to the information desk. "Has the bus from Yoder, Kansas, arrived yet?"

The guy checked his computer screen. "About twenty minutes ago."

Julia leaned into the counter. "Did you see a young boy, fourteen years old, brown hair, five-six and slender?"

The guy frowned. "Lady, do you know how many people come through this station each day?"

"He was wearing a gray Philadelphia Eagles sweatshirt."

"I didn't see him, ma'am, but that doesn't mean he wasn't here."

She turned away from the man who offered no help and pointed to a vending machine area. "Knowing William, he's probably hungry. I'll check the vending machines. You look in the restroom."

Julia was downcast when she met up with Abraham again. "You didn't find him either?"

"There is a fast-food restaurant at the end of the block."

Julia's spirits brightened. "He's probably eating a burger and fries. We need to hurry."

They walked rapidly along the street and soon arrived at the corner eatery. Julia peered through the tinted windows. The day was overcast, but the glare from the sun made it difficult to see inside.

"There." She spotted William. "He's at a table in the corner."

She hurried toward the door but stopped before she entered and grabbed Abraham's hand. "Pablo's inside. I don't think he's seen William yet. He's with another gang member from our neighborhood. His name's Mateo Gonzales."

Julia pointed out both guys to Abraham. Just as in

Philadelphia, they wore their gang's so-called uniform—white T-shirts, sagging pants, baseball caps turned backward and silk team jackets with *Philador* embroidered on one of the sleeves.

"You grab William and leave by that side door," Abraham said. "We passed a small inside shopping mall on the way here. Right hand side of the street, two blocks down. I will meet you there."

Abraham needed to distract Pablo and his buddy to give Julia time to grab William and hustle him out of the restaurant. If only the kid would go with her willingly and not give his mother a hard time.

Pablo elbowed Mateo and nodded in Julia's direction. Before Abraham could get around an elderly woman who stepped in front of him, Pablo grabbed Julia's arm.

She turned on him, eyes wide, and tried to pull her arm free. "No!" she cried.

A beefy guy, twice Pablo's size, stepped in front of him. "Hey, buddy. The lady doesn't want you touching her."

Pablo laughed nervously and dropped his hold. Mateo edged around the big guy and moved toward Julia. Abraham barreled into him, throwing him off balance.

Mateo fell back against a teenage girl. Her tray flew into the air, spilling French fries and a burger onto the floor. The plastic top sailed off her mega soft drink, spewing cola and ice.

A rush of customers came to the young woman's aid. In so doing, they surrounded Mateo and boxed him in.

Julia grabbed William. They left through a side door and hurried along the street, heading north to the rendezvous area Abraham had mentioned.

Disengaging himself from the gathering, he slipped

out the front door and crossed the street, hoping to throw off the gang members if they connected him with Julia or the boy.

He glanced back just as the two men hurried outside. They looked both directions and then split up. Pablo headed north. Mateo turned south toward the bus station. Abraham pretended to examine merchandise in a store window until Pablo passed by on the opposite side of the street.

The punk was medium height but built like a tank. More than likely, he had flown into Kansas City. From the bulge at his waist, he must have picked up a weapon on the street. The east side was known for gang activity where money could buy anything.

Pablo gazed into the stores he passed and entered a number of them. Each time, he quickly returned to the street and continued walking. A game arcade appeared ahead. The perfect place for a young teen with money in his pocket to pass the time.

Pablo glanced over his shoulder. Abraham slipped into an alleyway, fearing he had been seen. He counted to ten under his breath and then peered from his hiding spot. Pablo was gone. Probably into the arcade, searching for William.

Abraham sauntered along the sidewalk toward the arcade, peered through the window and then stepped inside the darkened interior. A strobe light twirled overhead and mixed with the flashing lights from the machines. A number of adults and a few teens dropped coins into slots and pressed buttons or pulled on levers that activated the various games, filling the arcade with pings and dings and all types of other sounds.

Abraham kept his head down and his gaze focused on the various patrons as he slowly circled through the rows of machines. At the rear of the arcade, he spied Pablo. The punk opened a door and slipped into an adjoining area.

Abraham's heart stopped. Pablo had gone from the game arcade through a back door into the shopping area where Julia and William would be waiting. Abraham's plan had backfired. He should have hurried to meet Julia instead of tailing Pablo. By now, the three of them could have been far from either Pablo or his friend. Instead, Julia and her son were in the gang member's crosshairs.

Abraham's police skills were rusty at best, but Julia and William were in danger, imminent danger, and Abraham needed to save them.

EIGHT

Julia spotted Pablo. She and William had been in a sporting goods store, trying to act nonchalant like the other shoppers all the while they stared at the door, waiting for Abraham. Only their Amish friend hadn't entered the store. Pablo had.

William tensed. "I'll talk to him, Mom, and tell him I'm not going with him."

"You will do nothing to alert him to your whereabouts, William. What don't you understand about being in danger?"

"Pablo was always nice to me. He's Davey's brother."

"And a member of the Philadores."

"Davey said he's getting out."

"Getting out so he can join another gang?" she asked.

"Maybe, but the other gang isn't looking for me, Mom."

"The Delphis want to get back at the Philadores. What better way than to capture the witness who can testify against the rival gang's leader? You'd be a pawn, William, a bargaining chip to be used by one gang against the other."

They'd keep her son alive as long as they needed him and then dispose of him once he was no longer of use.

She grabbed a pair of sweatpants off a rack, handed them to William and pushed him toward the dressing area. "Stay in the men's dressing room until I tell you to come out."

"Mom, you're getting carried away."

She leaned into his face. "I love you, William. I gave you life, and I will do anything to ensure you remain alive. Is that understood?"

He blinked.

"Get into the dressing room. Now. No arguments and don't come out until I give you the all clear."

Once William was gone, Julia glanced back at Pablo. He was walking through the shoe section, staring at the customers. Her heart stopped when he turned and started walking toward where she stood.

Julia grabbed a tennis outfit off a rack, slipped past a sales clerk who was arranging clothing on a nearby mannequin and hurried into the women's dressing area.

Heavy footsteps sounded behind her.

"Is anyone in there?" Pablo called into the dressing room from the entrance.

"Sir." A woman's voice. "I'm the sales clerk in charge of this area. Are you looking for someone?"

"My kid." Pablo grunted. "She's ten. I'm worried about her safety."

"We've never had a problem in this store. Wait out here, sir. I'll check the dressing rooms as soon as I help a customer find her size."

The click of high heels signaled the clerk had left to help her customer. Almost immediately, Pablo entered the changing area. Julia could see his shoes under the swinging, saloon-style door of the small dressing room where she hid. If she could see his feet, he could see hers. She climbed onto the ledge that doubled as a seat and held her breath. Her heart pounded like a jack hammer.

"Did you find your daughter, sir?" The click of high heels signaled the clerk's return. "Sir?"

The door to Julia's dressing room started to swing open.

"Men are not allowed in the women's changing area, sir." The clerk sounded indignant. "Leave now or I'll call security."

Pablo backed away from where Julia hid. "I'll check the guy's dressing room."

"Your daughter wouldn't go in there, sir. If you think there's a problem, I'll call security."

"Maybe she's in another store." He stomped off with the clerk clicking her heels after him.

Julia peered from the dressing area and spied Pablo heading to the front of the store.

"Mom?"

William was staring at her.

"What are you doing out here?" she demanded. "I told you to stay in the dressing room."

"Pablo was in the women's dressing room. I thought he'd come into the men's area next." William reached for her hand. "Come on, Mom. There's an emergency side exit."

Julia glanced at the front of the store. Seeing Pablo, she turned and hurried after her son. Just as he had said, there was an emergency exit. William pushed it open and stepped into a narrow passageway that ran behind the shops.

"Pablo won't find us here." He squeezed her hand. "We're safe."

"You were ready to go with Pablo not long ago. What changed your mind?"

"You did, Mom. You said you would do anything to

keep me alive. I don't think Pablo would hurt me, but I don't want to hurt you."

She put her hands on his shoulders and stared into his eyes. "Promise you'll never run away again and you'll never take money from my purse."

He hung his head and nodded. "I'll pay the money back."

The door they had just come through opened. Julia shoved William protectively behind herself.

A man stepped into the passageway.

She gasped, not from fear but with relief.

"Oh, Abraham, I didn't know if we'd ever see you again."

Abraham let out a deep sigh and pulled them both into his embrace. "I thought I had lost you."

"Did you see Pablo?"

"He left the mall and headed back toward the bus station. I just called Randy. We need to hurry to where he plans to meet us."

Abraham pointed to a side door that led to the street. "I will check outside and motion you both forward if the street is clear. Turn right, walk to the next intersection and make a left. The spot where Randy said he would be waiting will be at the end of the block."

He opened the door and stood for a long moment, eyeing the flow of traffic and the people on the street. Convinced that Pablo and Mateo were not in sight, Abraham motioned Julia and William forward. They turned right and then left at the intersection. Abraham looked repeatedly over his shoulder to ensure they were not being followed.

His heart pounded. They were too visible and so vulnerable. Any car driving by could see them, but Pablo and his buddy were on foot. At least, Abraham hoped they were.

The drive-through burger joint sat on the corner. Abraham's spirits took a nose dive as he studied the cars in the parking lot. The Amish taxi was nowhere to be seen.

"We could go inside, but I do not want a repeat of what happened at the restaurant earlier." He spotted a small, rundown hotel across the street that would provide a place to wait until the taxi appeared.

He hurried Julia and William to the corner and across the street once the light turned.

"Where are we going?" she asked.

"Into the hotel. We can wait inside and watch the flow of cars without being so conspicuous."

"What happened to Randy?"

"I am not sure. He might be held up in traffic."

"I'm worried, Abraham."

Abraham was worried too. Without transportation, they were trapped in the city with Pablo and his buddy, Mateo, searching for them.

NINE

Julia scooted closer to William. They both sat on a small settee in the hotel lobby while Abraham stood by the window, watching traffic. His last attempt to contact Randy had gone to voice mail.

The clerk at the desk had ignored them for almost an hour. Now he glanced repeatedly at them over his bifocals and finally asked, "You folks need a room?"

"We're waiting for someone," Julia said, offering a smile.

"Someone staying at the hotel?" the clerk asked.

"We're not sure."

Traffic on the street slowed to a standstill.

Abraham stepped toward Julia and lowered his voice. "Stay here while I phone Randy again. Maybe his cell phone is on by now."

He headed to the pay phone in the nearby alcove and returned some minutes later. "There is a problem with the taxi's engine," Abraham said under his breath. "Randy found a mechanic who called it a big job that will take hours. The guy said he would work late if Randy was willing to pay time and a half."

"Did Randy agree?"

"I told him I would cover the extra expense. I also talked to Jonathan and filled him in on what had happened. He was in his car, trying to get home. A spring snowstorm is blanketing Philadelphia, and his office is closed."

Julia's already faltering spirits plummeted even lower. "So, the US Marshals' office is brought to a halt by Mother Nature?" she whispered.

"Evidently."

The clerk cleared his throat. "I know you folks are watching for a friend of yours, but the lobby is reserved for hotel patrons only."

"I understand, sir." Abraham looked at Julia. "We will take two adjoining rooms."

She titled her head, confused.

"You and William can rest."

Which was a good plan. Her son's eyes were puffy and bloodshot. He probably hadn't slept last night nor on the bus ride to Kansas City.

Julia moved closer to the window as Abraham approached the registration desk to check them in.

An ambulance snaked through the traffic, its siren blaring.

Abraham turned to look at her.

She shrugged. "Maybe an accident."

"Any sign of Pablo or Mateo?"

Julia shook her head. "The only thing I see—"

Flicking her gaze to the far side of the street, she gasped and drew away from the window. She grabbed William's hand and motioned him to where Abraham stood by the registration desk. A phone rang in a back office. The clerk disappeared to answer the call.

"We've got a problem," Julia told Abraham, her voice low.

He glanced out the front window.

Pablo and Mateo were walking across the street toward the hotel.

"There's Davey's brother," William said, pointing to the picture window. "He's probably worried about me. Maybe I should tell him I'm with you, Mom, and not to worry."

She grabbed her son's arm. "You won't tell him anything, William. He and his friend came to Kansas City to find you and take you back to Philadelphia. They'll use you as a bargaining tool to improve their standing in one of the gangs."

Staring into William's troubled eyes, she added, "Don't you understand, son? Pablo doesn't care about you or your well-being. He's only thinking of himself."

"But I need to get a message to Davey."

"The only message you need to give anyone is that you're safely hidden, far from where any gang member can find you."

Abraham pointed to a side exit. "We need to leave the hotel."

Julia put her hand on William's shoulder. "Follow Abraham."

William glanced again through the large picture window. "They're coming inside, Mom."

"Go, William. Now."

Abraham grabbed William's arm and hurried him along a side hallway. Julia kept up with them, then looked back as the door into the hotel opened.

Just as the two men entered the lobby, Abraham and William turned into a side passageway. Julia ran after them. Abraham pushed on the door at the end of the corridor.

He looked back. His face tightened. "Hurry, Julia."

She glanced over her shoulder and saw Pablo. He called

to his friend and pointed to Julia. She followed Abraham and William out the door that slammed closed behind them.

"Down this alley." Abraham grabbed her hand and William's and hurried them along.

"Now left at the corner."

The street loomed ahead. They slowed to a fast walk so as not to draw attention and hurried around the corner.

"Cross the street, then turn right and left at the next corner."

Abraham glanced back. "Keep moving. Pablo and his friend are still in the alley."

Julia saw the fatigue that pulled at William's shoulders. She could tell from his eyes that he was frightened and tired.

"We need someplace to hole up," she said.

"What about there?" William pointed to a brick church on the next block.

"You think we should hide in the church?" Julia asked.

"In the basement, Mom. Some lady gave me a card in the bus station." He pulled it from his pocket. "The church has a night shelter for people who don't have a place to stay."

Abraham read over William's shoulder. "Fellowship Church Shelter opens at two. We need to hurry."

A small sign pointed to the rear of the church but when they rounded to the back of the property, Julia almost cried. A throng of people waited in line for the doors to open.

"Is it closed today?" she asked a woman standing in line.

"Opens at two. We've got a few minutes to wait."

"How many people do they take?"

"Thirty-five most days."

Julia started to count the people in the long line that snaked along the back of the church.

Abraham peered around the building in the direction from which they had just come. He moved closer to Julia. "Pablo and his friend are at the corner, heading this way."

If only the doors to the shelter would open and they could get inside. But as she counted off the number of people already in line, Julia's heart sank, realizing thirty-five people were ahead of them. They would be turned away and back on the street where Pablo would find them. She wrapped her arm around William's shoulder and grabbed Abraham's hand. They had to get inside.

The door to the shelter opened.

The woman admitting those in line was middle aged with a kind smile and understanding eyes. She welcomed many of the homeless as old friends and invited them in, and at the same time she gave them a number. Abraham stepped away for a minute and checked the street. His face was pulled tight when he returned to her side.

"You saw Pablo?" Julia asked.

"He is standing on the sidewalk just before the church, staring at the traffic."

"If he sees the sign for the shelter, he'll come around to the rear of the property and find us."

"You and William run if that happens. I'll try to slow him down."

"What if we're separated? Where can we meet up again?"

"Back at the corner where Randy said he would pick us up. Can you find it?"

"We'll try to get there."

The line moved slowly toward the back door.

"Welcome." The woman warmly greeted each person.

Julia stared at the side of the church, afraid she would see Pablo coming toward them.

Her heart stopped.

She could see his baseball cap over the fencing.

The woman counted to thirty-two. Three men stood between Julia, Abraham and William. The men would take the last spaces.

Tears burned Julia's eyes. "Please," she murmured.

She grabbed Abraham's hand and nodded toward the sidewalk where Pablo stood, looking back at the street.

The woman at the door of the shelter held up her hand. "Sorry, Norman, you and your friends can't stay here after the fight you started last week. I told you what would happen."

The three guys groused, but the woman held her ground. "Check with me next week and I'll see what I can do."

The men turned away and headed out along the sidewalk. Pablo started walking toward the rear of the church.

"Welcome," the woman said to Julia and Abraham with a wide smile as she handed them the last three numbers. "My name is Muriel. Make yourselves at home. Dinner will be served at five."

Julia hurried William inside.

"Restrooms," Abraham suggested, following close behind them. "William, come with me. We'll wait in the stalls in case Pablo comes into the shelter."

Julia hated to leave her son, but he was with Abraham. She had to trust they would remain safe. She hurried toward the ladies' room and glanced back as Pablo approached the door to the shelter, demanding entry.

"Sir, you're not allowed to be here." Muriel barred his entrance. "This is an overnight shelter for people who don't have a place to stay. We don't accept anyone who cuts in line or tries to force themselves inside."

Pablo grumbled, but he walked away.

Julia let out a sigh of relief. They had found shelter in the church, at least for the moment.

Abraham and William stepped out from the restroom. Abraham stared at her, his gaze cutting into her heart. He had tried to live a peaceful life after his daughter and wife had been killed. He had offered Julia and her children shelter out of the goodness of his heart. He didn't deserve anything bad to befall him.

Keep him safe, Lord, Julia prayed. *Keep us all safe.*

Abraham motioned them to a sofa in the corner of the large central common area where Julia and William could relax. The boy's eyes drooped soon after they sat down. He placed his head on Julia's shoulder and within a few minutes he had drifted to sleep. Julia rested her head against the back of the seat and closed her eyes. Every so often, she blinked her eyes open and peered at the various people gathered in the basement area.

A number of the men were middle-aged with graying hair. They shuffled as they walked and chatted amicably with some of the others gathered. The homeless women stayed in a corner, talking softly among themselves. A number of volunteers worked in the kitchen, preparing the meal they would soon serve. Showers were available and the homeless signed up for a time slot.

The woman who had greeted them at the door came by and smiled at the sight of William sleeping on Julia's shoulder.

"We're glad you're here," Muriel said to Abraham.

"Thank you, ma'am."

"You and your family are most welcome."

Family?

He started to correct her but stopped himself. He wanted to tell her his family had been murdered by a man who sought revenge for being incarcerated.

For too long, Abraham had felt that same desire for revenge against the man who had planted the explosive in Abraham's car. He should have been the one to die and not his precious daughter and beautiful wife. The memory of all that had happened cut through him again and opened the wound he tried to keep bandaged. Today he felt raw. Maybe because he had not been able to help Julia and William.

What was wrong with him? He had wanted to find the boy and take him back to Yoder, but they were holed up in a homeless shelter with two punk gang members looking for them on the street. Abraham had lost his edge. He had gone soft and was an ineffective protector.

Turning to gaze at Julia and William, his heart warmed. The boy had been obstinate and had made a huge mistake in calling his friend and running away, but he was basically a good kid. The hurt and anger he carried seemed aimed at his father. If only Will could realize how much his mother loved him and how much she had sacrificed to keep him safe. Maybe then he would understand the danger he was in and see the Philadores for who they truly were.

As she slept, the worry lines on Julia's face softened and she appeared more peaceful than Abraham had seen her thus far. Her eyes fluttered open and his chest constricted. He did not expect to react to the emotion that soared through him for one brief moment.

She pulled herself upright, smoothed her sweater and then tugged her hand through her hair. She glanced at William, still asleep, his head still on her shoulder.

"I must have dozed off."

"Rest longer, Julia. We seemed to have found a good place to wait until the taxi is fixed."

"You'll call Randy?"

"If I can find a phone. Randy said the mechanic would work until eleven. We will know then if we have to spend the night here or whether we can meet up with Randy."

Julia glanced at the kitchen. "Something smells good."

"You must be hungry."

"A little." She brushed the hair out of William's eyes and smiled at her sleeping son. "I'm sure he'll enjoy dinner, too."

Abraham went to the far side of the basement and peered out the window. Traffic was still bad. Hopefully Pablo and his friend had moved on. They would not give up, of that he could be certain. He had to get Julia and William out of the city and back to Yoder and the safety of the Amish community.

The woman who had welcomed them was wiping down the tables for dinner. Abraham approached her. "Ma'am, is there a pay phone at the shelter?"

She stopped working and smiled. "You're new here."

"It is our first time."

"How long have you been on the street?"

"Just today. We are traveling and ran into some difficulty."

"I know a construction company that hires day laborers if you're willing to work."

"I appreciate the offer, ma'am, but we plan to leave as soon as our ride can get here, today or tonight."

"We have beds if you need a place to sleep." She pointed to doors that led out of the common area to the right and the left. "Women on one side, men on the other. Your son will need to stay with you. We provide bedding and showers as well as breakfast in the morning."

"You provide a much-needed ministry."

"Just doing the Lord's work." She tilted her head. "Are you a believer?"

"I am."

She nodded. "I could tell. Glad you're here. Stay as long as you like."

"Thank you, ma'am. What about the pay phone?"

"A door on each side of this common area leads to a hallway outside the men's and women's dorm rooms. You'll find the phones there."

"Thank you." Abraham pushed through the swinging door, relieved to see the phones.

Randy's voice was tense when he answered. "I'm with the mechanic. He's working as fast as he can, but I still don't know when he'll finish. Can I reach you on this phone?"

"You can try calling. I might hear it ring, but I cannot say for sure."

"Then you call me, Abraham."

"I appreciate all you have done, Randy."

"You've been a friend for a lot of years, right?"

"*Yah*, since we were boys."

"I liked your *datt*. He was a good man. A bit pigheaded at times, but still a good man. The least I can do is help his son."

Julia's eyes blinked open when Abraham settled into the chair next to her.

"You don't look happy," she said. "Evidently Randy didn't provide good news."

"The mechanic continues to work on the problem. I will call again later."

"I'm not sure staying here is a good idea."

"We could try the hotel," he suggested.

She held up her hand. "Just kidding. The shelter works for me. I wonder if the hotel clerk told Pablo that his friends had been waiting for him."

"Maybe. The clerk made it clear he did not like us hanging around. At least here we are welcome."

"And fed."

"I can see the street from the window at the front of the church. Traffic is still bad."

"Did you see Pablo?"

"I did not."

"Would I be too optimistic to think he might have left town?"

"Yes." Abraham smiled. "Much too optimistic. My guess is that he will remain in this area at least until tomorrow."

She nodded. "When the children and I were trying to get away from Charlie, I considered staying at a shelter for a night or two. Somehow I was always able to scrape up enough money for a hotel. Not necessarily the nicest of hotels, but we were together in a room, and I could watch over both children. Most of the shelters, like this one, divide the men and women into two areas so William would have been taken away from me. I couldn't bear for that to happen."

"He will have to sleep in the men's dorm tonight, Julia, but I will be there with him."

"I know and I appreciate all you've done for us, Abraham."

"I am not sure if I have helped or hurt your chances of getting free of the Philadores."

"Why do you say that?"

"Because you are being hunted still."

"But this time we're not alone. You are with us, Abraham, to guide us."

"You have needed no guidance except at which corner to turn."

She laughed. William stirred. He blinked his eyes open and glanced at both of them before he drifted back to sleep.

"When I checked my purse earlier, I found a note Mrs. Fielding had given me when we were in Philadelphia."

"The lady who lived in your apartment building?" he asked.

"That's right. She watched the children for me when I worked at a neighborhood diner."

Julia opened her purse and pulled out a piece of folded notepaper. "It's a short prayer Mrs. Fielding said whenever she was worried or in trouble. *Jesus, I trust in You.*"

"Sounds like she was a woman of faith."

"Indeed. She'd been through hard times. Her husband died some years back. They'd lost a son to a drug overdose, but she kept her faith and her trust in the Lord. She taught me a lot about believing in God's abundant mercy."

"When Marianne and Becca died, I railed at God and blamed Him for their deaths. I did not want to live and could not understand why I had been the one to live."

"Jonathan said a paroled criminal was trying to get back at you for arresting him."

"He thought I would be driving the car instead of my wife. Her car needed an oil change. I took it to the mechanic that morning so she would not have to deal with the problem."

The memory of kissing Marianne goodbye before he had left the house flooded over him. Becca had run from her room and grabbed his legs. He had lifted her into his arms and kissed her cheek. She had wrapped her arms around his neck and giggled. The last words he had heard from her sweet mouth were "Daddy, I love you."

Julia reached out her hand and took his. "Losing those we love, especially an innocent child, is the hardest thing anyone has to do. God watched His son suffer and die on the cross, Abraham. He understands your pain."

"That is what Jonathan tried to make me realize. He was there when I needed him."

"Which is why you took us into your home. I'm very grateful, and I'm also sorry that you had to leave your peaceful farm to help me find my son."

Abraham offered a weak smile. "William is a good boy. He has been hurt and feels abandoned by his father. That is a hard place for a boy to be."

"I know you were a good father, Abraham. I can tell by the way you interact with Kayla and William."

"Kayla never met a stranger, as the saying goes."

Julia nodded. "Which is not always good. Plus, she's wise beyond her years. I'm glad we left Philadelphia. It wasn't a good environment. I tried to keep the children at home as much as possible, but that's not the best, either. I kept blaming Charlie for everything that had happened, yet I was the one who married him. That mistake was totally mine."

"You have two wonderful children, so good came from your marriage."

"That's true. I'm blessed beyond words, thanks to them."

William stirred again and blinked open his eyes. "Did you say something?" he asked.

"Only that I'm glad you're my son."

The boy smiled. "I...I'm sorry about running away."

"Right now we need to give thanks for finding you and

for keeping you safe." She glanced at Abraham. "We have someone to thank for that."

William hung his head and then glanced up. His gaze was sincere when he spoke. "Thank you both for coming after me. I wasn't thinking about anyone but myself, like you said back in the barn, Abraham. I was wrong."

"*Yah*, we have all made mistakes. This one will end well. You have a lifetime ahead of you, William, and much for which to be thankful. You are a good young man. You will grow into a strong man who makes good decisions."

"Do you really think so?" The boy seemed hungry for affirmation.

"I know it is so."

A bell rang. The woman who had welcomed them stepped to the middle of the room. "The meal will be served soon. Let us give thanks, then if you want to wash up before eating, the restrooms are on either side of the living area."

She waited for everyone to settle and then bowed her head. "Dear God, we thank You for all those who are here today. We ask Your blessing on each of them, on the volunteers and on the generous people who provided the food for this meal. Touch each person with Your love and with Your mercy. Allow us to place our trust in You, Lord. Amen."

Julia nodded. "Amen,"

"A good prayer," Abraham said.

"And another confirmation about the importance of trust."

William took her hand. "You can trust me, Mom." He looked at Abraham. "I learned an important lesson."

"*Yah*, to trust *Gott* and those who love you. You need to also trust yourself, William. This will come with time."

Abraham glanced at the people who were headed to

the wash area. "Now, let us prepare to eat. I know you are hungry."

William nodded. "I am starving. I could eat a cow."

Abraham laughed. "You have ambition, William."

"That's good, isn't it?" the boy asked.

"Yes, William. It is very *gut*."

TEN

Julia hadn't realized how hungry she was until she went through the food line. When a server asked if anyone wanted seconds, both Abraham and William went back for another helping of meat loaf and green beans. William asked for more bread and received an extra dollop of whipped butter to put on the homemade rolls.

An assortment of desserts was on a side table, which interested Julia. The gut-wrenching fear that had hovered over her for so long had lifted, and she was relieved they were in what seemed like a secure environment, at least for the evening.

The older men—regulars, as Muriel called them—took a liking to William. A number of them reached out to her son and encouraged him to get his education and a good job so he could do something worthwhile with his life. The regulars weren't speaking poorly of those in the shelter but rather bolstering William's morale and letting him know that he could dream big dreams and follow his heart.

After everyone had eaten, Muriel asked William to help her clear the tables. Instead of rejecting the offer, he eagerly jumped up and started to work. Julia and Abraham both offered to help, but she insisted the kitchen was in good hands.

"You folks relax. We have a number of volunteers. We'll let them do the work, along with William. I thought he might enjoy being of service." She patted Julia's hand. "You have a good boy there. He'll make you proud someday."

The woman's words touched Julia's heart. For too long, she had worried about William's future. Having pride in her son was something she had not even dared imagine.

She watched him follow Muriel to the kitchen and felt a swell of optimism in her heart. Things were starting to change, which gave her hope.

"I never thought my son would flourish in a shelter," she told Abraham. "If I had realized how much he enjoyed working with folks who were down and out, we might have visited them earlier."

"It does seem that he has had a change of heart, Julia. Once we get back to Yoder, I will assign him jobs to do. He showed an interest in Buttercup and was eager to work in the barn—even mucking out the stalls did not seem to bother him. Being successful at small tasks in the beginning will build his self-confidence. Once he becomes proficient at the initial jobs, others will be added. You will see a change in him within the month."

If only what Abraham said would prove true. She thought back over the last few years when the future had seemed so hopeless. Mrs. Fielding had prayed for them, and in her own way, Julia had sought help from the Lord. Although she'd never thought He heard her prayers. Maybe she hadn't been patient enough. Plus she never would have imagined the Lord could provide what William needed in not only a distant state but also in a homeless shelter with an Amish man who had cut himself off from the world.

She glanced at Abraham as he walked to the far end of the common area and peered out the window. His height and build always surprised Julia, as if she could never remember how strong and big he really was until he stepped away from her and she saw him from a distance.

He was handsome in a clean, outdoorsy way, a wholesome look that made her heart flutter when he glanced over his shoulder and caught her staring at him. She should not be thinking of his looks or his strength at this particular time. She should be focused on protecting her son instead of thinking about the man who made her heart skip a beat.

Looking around, she studied the other men. No one came close to having Abraham's charisma. Her cheeks burned and she shook her head ever so slightly, needing to focus on something else instead of on Abraham.

Once the kitchen was tidy, the men gathered at various tables and played chess and checkers. William joined in the fun. The men enjoyed his enthusiasm and a number of them patted his back when he made good plays and captured his opponent's pieces.

Julia glanced at the window, seeing the night fall, and thought of Kayla. Although she knew her daughter was well cared for, she still hated to be away from her.

Keep her safe, Lord, she prayed. *Let no harm come to my sweet little one.*

By nine o'clock, Julia knew many of the people would head to the dorm rooms soon to claim their beds. She didn't want to leave Abraham and William.

"Perhaps we can stay in this common area tonight," she said.

"You need a bed, Julia. The couch worked for a short nap, but for a longer sleep you need to lie down."

Muriel approached them. "I placed a reserved sign on two of the cots near the entrance and close to the hallway and the phones, Abraham. I know you've been waiting for a call."

"From the man who will drive us home," Julia said.

"You're welcome to stay out here for a while. By ten-thirty, we ask that everyone retire to the dorm areas."

"Thank you for providing such a lovely shelter and the delicious dinner," Julia said. "Your hospitality and understanding have touched us deeply."

"The Lord calls all of us to welcome the stranger and to feed the hungry. You'll take what you received here and pass it on to others in your lives who will need help at another time. I sec great love between you all." Muriel's smile was warm and sincere.

Julia looked down, unable to face Abraham. He was a good man, thrown into this situation due to his own desire to help another person in need. He had not realized what saying yes to Jonathan would entail.

"We will try to reach out as beautifully as you have done, ma'am." Abraham stood. "I need to make another phone call in case the car is ready."

He entered the dorm area. Muriel patted Julia's hand. "He is a good man. I do not see a ring on your finger so I presume you are not married. This is something you should consider."

Embarrassed by the woman's words, Julia shook her head. "It's not what you think. He is helping me escape a bad situation, and regrettably, we have pulled him into the danger that surrounds us."

"He cares for you. I can see it in his eyes."

"Maybe you see his inability to leave us. Two gang members are after my son."

"Which gang?"

"The Philadores."

The manager nodded. “I’ve heard of them, but they aren’t prevalent in the local area.”

Muriel glanced at a couple of men sitting in the far corner of the room. “Grant’s the guy with the scar on his face. He was a gang member until he found Jesus. Now he tries to help the kids get off the street.”

“Yet he’s homeless himself?”

“He calls himself a vagabond for the Lord. He might know a way to get you safely out of town and away from the Philadores.”

“I’m not sure you should mention our situation to him. I probably said more than I should have.”

“Don’t worry. Grant can be trusted. I would do nothing to place you or your son in danger.”

Muriel did as she had mentioned and talked quietly with Grant. The man put down the newspaper he was reading and approached Julia. “Muriel told me about your problem with the Philador gang. That’s a presence no one wants to have get a foothold in Kansas City. We have our own problems with gangs and do not need more bad actors stealing our youth and wreaking havoc in our city.”

“I’m sorry that we might have brought them here.”

“Do you have a picture of the gang members?”

“No, but their names are Pablo Davila and Mateo Gonzales.” She described what they were wearing.

“The Philadores usually have a script *P* tattooed on their left hands.”

“Yes.” Julia nodded. “That’s correct. Pablo has one. I’m not sure about Mateo.”

“They wish to harm your son, Muriel told me, which means he’s seen something or knows something that could cause them problems.”

Julia refused to comment on Grant’s last statement. She had already told him more than she should. Instead, she said, "The two men have been searching for us on the street. We need to meet a car as soon as it gets out of the mechanic's shop, but I fear we will be seen and followed."

"What time are you leaving here?"

She shrugged. "That depends on how fast the mechanic works."

"A few hours?" he asked.

She glanced at the clock on the wall. "The mechanic said he would keep working until eleven. If the work isn't completed by then, he'll have to finish the job tomorrow."

"Everyone has to leave the shelter in the morning by eight." Grant pursed his full lips. "Muriel needs time to have the place cleaned and the sheets washed before the doors open again at two tomorrow afternoon."

Julia signed. Eight o'clock seemed early. Where would they go? "I don't want to think about being on the street again tomorrow."

"Then let's hope your mechanic gets the job done."

Abraham hurried back into the room and looked concerned when he saw Grant talking to Julia.

She introduced her new acquaintance and tried to sooth Abraham's unease. "This gentleman knows some of the local gangs. He tries to get kids off the street. I told him two Philadores were searching for us."

Abraham's gaze narrowed. "I hope you are a trustworthy man, Grant. Julia seems to think you can help us, instead of doing us harm."

"I'll make a few phone calls. Let me know before you head onto the street. I'll see if the people I know can provide some cover for you."

Abraham stared at him for a long moment and then stretched out his hand. The two men shook. "Any help you can provide will be greatly appreciated."

Grant glanced first at where William sat playing chess, then back at Julia. His wide smile touched her heart.

"Your boy has made an impact on a number of people here this evening," Grant said. "We see some kids, but usually they stay to themselves and don't wish to interact. Your son has a big heart."

"You can thank his mother for that," Abraham added. "She has raised him well."

Grant nodded. "A mother's love makes all the difference." He turned to Abraham. "Young men also need strong fathers who can guide their sons and be a role model for them. You've done a good job yourself."

Abraham started to object, but Julia shook her head.

If Grant considered Abraham the father of her child, she didn't want anyone to set him straight. Abraham had all the qualities that would make a good father and William seemed drawn to him. If only they could stay with Abraham long enough for William to get on his feet and directed to the right path.

"I'll make those phone calls now." Grant stood. "Let me know before you leave."

Once he returned to his seat on the far side of the room, Abraham scooted closer to Julia. "I hope we can trust him."

"We need help, Abraham. Muriel mentioned that Grant could be of assistance. We have to trust him."

Trust. What Julia struggled to accept in her own life. Perhaps being with Abraham was also rubbing off on her.

Muriel blinked the lights. "It's time to put the games away so we can pray together before everyone gets a good night's sleep."

The men did as she asked. Working together, they returned the board games and magazines and books to the cupboards.

"We close each day with night prayer," Muriel said once the room was tidy. "I hope you'll all join us."

She looked around the room. "Who would like to read the scripture to us this evening?"

Most of the people glanced down as if unwilling to volunteer. She nodded to Julia and then Abraham.

He stood and walked to the Bible and read from Psalm 33. The verse, "Let thy mercy, O Lord, be upon us, according as we hope in thee," resonated with Julia.

Hope and trust were similar. Was the Lord telling her something and speaking to her heart? Could she trust the Lord? Was He telling her she could also trust Abraham?

Muriel prayed a blessing over all of them for the night ahead, for their safety, for peace and for an end to misery and heartache.

The prayer seemed aimed directly at Julia.

"Amen," they all said in unison.

She hugged William. "Stay with Abraham. I'll be in the other dorm room."

"Don't worry, Mom. I won't run away again."

She looked into his eyes and saw the truthfulness of his statement. "I trust you, William, and I love you."

Abraham waited nearby. "Do not worry," he told her when William stepped out of her embrace. "I will have Muriel contact you if Randy calls tonight."

"Thank you, Abraham. Keep William safe."

But when he and her son headed to the men's dorm, she started thinking of what could happen. What if someone broke in and found them? What if Grant warned the other gang members and they worked with the Philadores? What if the safety of this shelter wasn't real?

Muriel stepped toward her. "You're worried. I see it written on your face."

"Leaving my son is hard."

"I'll be up for a few more hours and promise to wake you if something changes."

"I hate to act like I'm not grateful, Muriel. It's just that so much has happened."

"Have you given it to God?"

Julia didn't understand.

"Give Him your worries and your fears. Give Him your son. After all we're all God's children. His love is unconditional so we know He loves William even more than you do, and He wants only good for all of us. Trust in the Lord, Julia. Let Him carry the burdens that weigh you down now. He can handle everything perfectly and in His perfect time."

"I have problems trusting Him, Muriel. He turned away from me when I was in need."

"Did the Lord turn away from you or did you turn away from Him, which is usually the case?"

"I'm not sure." Julia hesitated for a moment. "You've given me something to think about."

"Well, tonight try not to think about anything. Just get some rest. Things will seem better in the morning."

If only that would be true.

ELEVEN

Muriel woke Julia in the night. She hurried to join Abraham and William in the main room. Grant was there, cautioning Abraham to wait inside the shelter until the older man received a phone call.

Randy had called. He had paid the mechanic even more money to keep working past the eleven o'clock cutoff.

William looked tired and worried. He'd changed out of his sweatshirt into a dark jacket and baseball cap Muriel had provided so he wouldn't be recognized.

Shouts sounded from the street.

"What's going on?" Julia asked Abraham.

"The gangs are rallying. Seems someone warned them that the Philadores were infiltrating the city and ready to start up a group here."

"What about Pablo and Mateo?"

"They are outside somewhere. Grant's getting us an escort to the intersection where Randy will meet us."

Muriel gave Julia a small bag. "I made sandwiches for all of you and added some cookies and water. You'll need food once you get to your car."

"You've thought of everything."

Muriel turned to glance at Grant. "You've had help from some good people this evening. It's going to work out."

Grant's phone rang. He pulled it to his ear and nodded. "Thanks."

He pocketed his phone and approached Abraham. "It's time. My contacts spotted Pablo and Mateo. The description you gave was perfect. They'll keep them occupied while you slip outside and down the street. An escort will be waiting at the corner. They'll ensure you don't have trouble meeting your ride."

"Thanks, Grant."

"Just trying to help. Pass it on, like Muriel always tells us."

Julia squeezed his hand. "We will."

She hugged Muriel.

"Go with God," the woman said.

Julia grabbed William's hand. Abraham ushered them toward the door. She glanced back to see Muriel's encouraging smile. Grant gave them a thumbs-up as Abraham opened the door and slipped into the cool night. He motioned them forward.

The door shut behind them. Rounding the corner of the church, Julia gasped, seeing the swarms of teens and twentysomethings gathered. Their taunts made her heart race, fearing a fight was about to ensue.

She pulled William close to her side. What had she done to place her child in danger? Abraham had said they could get away without being stopped, but heading into the middle of a gang fight was asking for trouble that could end up badly for all of them. She should have stayed in the shelter with William.

"Hurry, Julia." Abraham motioned her forward. "We only have a short window of time to get to the intersection where we will meet Randy." He held out his hand to her. "Trust me."

If only she could.

* * *

Fear flashed in Julia's eyes. Abraham's heart went out to her for the situation there were in. All she wanted to do was keep her son safe, yet they were walking into the middle of what appeared to be a clash between two street gangs. They were taking a big risk that could turn deadly.

"We have to keep walking." Abraham put his hand on Julia's shoulder and guided her forward. She scooted William closer to Abraham so the boy would be protected between both of them.

"Keep your head down," Abraham said. "We will slip out along the side of the road. Act nonchalant."

William looked as frightened as his mother. If they got out of this alive, the boy might understand the reality of being in a gang and change his mind about having anything to do with the Philadores.

The shouts on the street escalated. Abraham walked on the outside to protect Julia and William. Once they rounded the church, they stayed on the sidewalk, keeping their eyes averted so they would not make eye contact with any of the punks who might want to have fun at their expense.

"What about Pablo and Mateo?" Julia whispered.

"Grant said the people he called had spotted them."

Julia glanced over her shoulder. "Pablo and his buddy are on the far side of the street." Her voice was shaky and laced with fear.

"Keep walking." Abraham wanted to look back as Julia had done, but he would not risk Pablo seeing him.

"Hey, you!" someone shouted.

"Stay calm," Abraham cautioned.

"Pablo must have seen us," Julia whispered.

"Just keep walking. If I say run, you and William head to the intersection where Randy will be waiting."

"We won't go without you," William said.

The boy's words touched Abraham's heart. "You have to get your mom out of danger, William. I will stay back and distract anyone who tries to follow you. Can you protect her?"

"I can try."

"Hey, you guys." The voice came again.

Abraham glanced back. Two men were heading straight for them.

"Grant sent us," the taller of the two men said as they approached. "The Philadores who followed you are being detained by some of our local guys. We'll stay with you until we get to a safer area."

A gunshot rang out. Abraham's heart stopped.

"Sounds like things have gone south," one of the guys said. "Let's pick up the pace."

Abraham, Julia and William started to run. Grant's friends followed close behind.

"Cross here," one of them said. "The street's clear."

Sirens sounded in the distance. More volleys of gunfire. "Did Grant order the violence?" Abraham asked.

"No way, man. Grant's cool. He works to keep peace in the hood. It's the local gangs. They're fighting for their own turf. That area around the shelter can get bad. We watch out for Muriel, and Grant calls us in if anything comes too close to the shelter. Tonight, we didn't expect gunfire."

The other man pointed to an alleyway. "Head between those buildings, it leads to the intersection. Grant said you need to meet your driver there."

Abraham glanced at Julia, worried that the pace was too much for her. She was keeping up but winded and, from the look on her face, scared to death.

William stayed close to his mom as if he was taking to heart Abraham's suggestion to protect her.

The alley was narrow and the main road appeared ahead. Traffic whizzed by. Abraham hoped they would be able to find Randy.

One of the guys held up his hand. “Wait here. I’ll check the street.”

Julia leaned into Abraham. He put his hand on her shoulder.

“Did we escape without Pablo seeing us?” she asked.

“I hope so.”

“A car just pulled to the curb,” the guy announced. “Looks like your ride has arrived.”

Abraham squeezed Julia’s shoulder. “Let me go first.” But when he peered around the corner, his heart stopped. He did not recognize the car or the man sitting behind the wheel.

“Wrong car. We will wait in the alley.”

“Is it the gang member who’s after you?” Grant’s friend asked.

Abraham shook his head. “Someone new.”

“We’ll check it out.”

Grant’s friends walked toward the street and stopped near the car. They started laughing and making a ruckus, which gave Abraham a chance to study the car and driver. Finally, the vehicle drove off.

Abraham let out a deep breath.

Grant’s friends returned. “I don’t know who the driver was, but he had a Glock sitting in the passenger seat.”

Julia grabbed Abraham’s hand. “It could have been someone from the Philadores.”

Abraham spied Randy’s car across the street. “There is our ride.”

He turned to the two men and shook their hands. “Thanks, guys. You saved us.”

"Hey, you're a friend of Grant's. That's all we need to know."

"We appreciate the escort and help. I doubt we would have made it here unharmed without you."

Their new friends looked up and down the street. "Get going now. The street's clear. Things could change in a heartbeat."

Abraham ushered Julia and William across the roadway. He opened the back door of the Amish taxi, and they all slipped into the rear.

"Do you know how glad we are to see you?" he asked Randy as he closed the door and buckled his seat belt.

Randy laughed. "The feeling's mutual. This city isn't for me, Abraham. Let's get outta here."

Gunshots echoed. "Sounds as if things haven't calmed down near the shelter," Julia said, glancing back.

"Stay down," Abraham warned. "Until we are out of this area."

Randy pulled onto the main road. Another car pulled in behind them. Abraham glanced over his shoulder. "That looks like the sedan that was parked on the road earlier. The driver has a Glock on the seat next to him, Randy. Probably a nine millimeter strapped to his hip. He might have an ankle holster, as well. See if you can lose him."

Randy accelerated.

"Who is it?" Julia asked, her voice tight.

"No clue."

Randy increased his speed even more.

"Hang a left at the next intersection," Abraham suggested.

The light started to change. Randy accelerated through the yellow and turned left. The car behind them was forced to stop.

"Hit it, Randy."

Traffic was light, and Randy pushed down on the accelerator, but before long Abraham spotted the car again.

They needed to dump the tail. "Take a right and a left. See if you can lose him."

Randy nodded and followed Abraham's promptings. Eventually they ended up on a four-lane boulevard lined with homes.

Before they had gone more than half a mile, the car reappeared behind them.

"The guy's sticking like glue," Randy said.

Julia groaned. "I'm scared, Abraham."

"Wc are in good hands with Randy at the wheel, Julia. We will get through this."

"You're sure?" she asked.

"Absolutely."

But he was not sure of anything, especially since the tail kept coming after them.

More sirens. Two police cars flew past, heading in the opposite direction.

Randy turned on the car radio and found the news.

"Police are advising everyone to stay clear of the area near the Fellowship Church Shelter," the radio news commentator said. "Fighting has broken out between rival gangs. At this point, there are two confirmed dead with a number of life-threatening injuries."

"What about the men who helped us?" Julia said. "I pray they weren't hurt."

"They seemed to know their way around the city. My hunch is they stayed clear of the violence."

"What about Grant and Muriel?" William asked.

"From what Grant said, the church is a neutral zone. I doubt anyone holed up inside would be hurt. The fighting would have been on the street."

Randy turned off the radio and glanced over his shoulder. "I don't see the car."

"Which worries me," Abraham admitted.

"Do we cross the bridge and head west or chill around here and kill time?"

"Bad choice of words," Abraham said with a wry smile. "Your call."

"Take the bridge."

Randy pulled into the turn lane and rounded the curve aimed toward the water. Abraham glanced over his shoulder and stared behind them.

"See anything?" Randy asked.

"Headlights, but I am not sure about the car."

"Traffic on the bridge is light, which is good."

The headlights were catching up to them. "Check the right-hand lane."

Randy nodded. "Our tail doesn't realize we're exiting. Hold on, everyone."

The car sped along the exit ramp.

Abraham grabbed the front seat to keep from slamming against the door.

William groaned.

"You doing okay over there?" Abraham asked.

"Even with my seatbelt buckled, I crashed into Mom."

"No harm done," she said. "Although I'd like to straighten up."

"Keep your head down a few minutes more, Julia."

Abraham patted Randy's back as they crossed the bridge to the Kansas side of the city without their tail.

"That is what I call too close for comfort." Randy let out a deep sigh and eased up on the gas.

Abraham looked back again to ensure they truly were free of the tail before he helped Julia straighten up.

"Are you okay?" he asked.

"A little shaken but no harm done."

She looked at William. "What about you, hon?"

"I'm okay, Mom."

"Sure?"

"Just worried about Grant."

"Grant knows how to take care of himself," Abraham said. "Plus he has friends who work with him seemingly for good. You need not worry, William, but instead offer a prayer of gratitude that God led us to the shelter."

Julia took her son's hands and both of them closed their eyes for a long moment. Abraham silently lifted up his own words of thanks to the Lord.

He smiled at Julia when she opened her eyes, but she was not smiling. She was tense and scared.

If they could get out of the city and onto the back roads, everyone could relax. It had been three years since he left law enforcement. Some days he had longed to put on his badge again, but being with Julia and fearing for her safety, as well as William's, made him realize he was well ensconced in the Amish life and farming. He no longer wanted to fight crime.

Abraham wanted peace and tranquility, but he did not want the loneliness that he often felt on the farm. Julia and William and Kayla had awakened a need within him for companionship. He glanced at Julia. She had closed her eyes, her arm around William who rested his head on her shoulder.

Abraham had feelings for Julia and her children, although he could not put a name to those feelings. But he cared about them and he was relieved that they were headed back to Yoder. He prayed trouble would not follow them.

TWELVE

Randy turned the car radio back on to the easy listening station, but even with the restful music, Julia's pulse continued to race. Mentally she knew they were safe, at least for now, but knowing what had happened and the memory of how close they had come to being caught in the middle of two warring gangs circled through her mind.

William's breathing became shallow as he drifted to sleep. A swell of gratitude rose within her for all Abraham had done to keep them safe. A warmth filtered over her as he turned to her, his eyes filled with concern.

"I thought you were asleep," he said in a soft voice so as not to wake William or distract Randy.

"Just grateful we made it out of the city."

He nodded. "I will call Jonathan and let him know."

"Tell him you kept us safe."

"We worked together, Julia. I will tell Jonathan we make a good team."

"He asked you to take care of us because he knew you were a good man, Abraham." She smiled and then glanced at her son. "I hope William has learned his lesson. He was more frightened than I've ever seen him. Plus, Grant made a good impression on him, along with Muriel."

"William made a good impression on them. He is a fine boy, Julia. Your hard work has paid off."

Abraham's words brought comfort. "For so long I didn't know if William believed what I was telling him," she said. "The street was a bigger draw than staying home with his mom and sister. I was afraid I would lose him."

"But you did not lose him. Even when he ran away, you were able to find him."

"Because of you, Abraham. If not for you, I would have lost my son."

He took her hand and held it as the car traveled along the back roads. Julia's pulse calmed and the tension that had gripped her eased. Abraham had come to her rescue. He had arranged for Randy to drive them, for Kayla to be cared for by Sarah and for ways to keep them away from the Philador gang in Kansas City. Julia would always be grateful.

Once they were out of the city, Abraham called Jonathan on Randy's phone. He kept his voice low to keep from being heard by the taxi driver. "We are heading back to Yoder," Abraham told Jonathan.

"That's good news. You have William?"

"We do. We holed up in a church shelter not far from the bus station. A woman named Muriel runs the shelter in the basement of the Fellowship Church. Turns out some former gang members, who found the Lord and work to get kids off the street, came to our aid and arranged an escort. They got us to where we had arranged to meet our taxi."

"You had the marshal's office in Kansas City worried."

Abraham pushed the phone close to his ear. "Did you contact them?"

"They sent a man to pick you up at the intersection where you planned to connect with Randy. The marshal followed you for a short time but eventually lost you."

Abraham smiled to himself. "The guy was driving a black Buick."

"You saw him?"

Abraham glanced at Randy, grateful that he was focused on the road, and lowered his voice even more. "And the Glock he had on his passenger seat. We thought he was associated with the Philadores."

"Since when does a US Marshal look like a street thug?"

"After everything that happened, we did not hang around to ask questions."

"I'm sorry we couldn't be more help. We'll all breathe more easily once you're back at the farm."

Abraham would, too. He was ready for the danger to end, although Julia and her children would be looking over their shoulders for years to come. Would it ever end?

Abraham thought again of the people they had met at the shelter. Muriel was a good woman who helped so many. As Grant had mentioned, Abraham would endeavor to pay forward the outreach that had benefitted them. Many people were down and out. Instead of being reclusive and only interested in his own needs, Abraham vowed to get out more and help others.

Right now he was helping Julia, but she would not remain on his farm forever, much as he enjoyed having her and her family stay with him.

He turned to stare out the window and thought about what he had lost and what had returned to his life.

Could Julia ever fill the void left by his wife?

She could. In fact, she had already done so.

THIRTEEN

Julia blinked her eyes open when Randy turned the taxi onto the road leading to Sarah's house. She rubbed her eyes and sat up straighter.

"I hope we don't frighten Sarah, knocking at her door at this hour."

Abraham patted her hand. "She should be expecting us."

The house sat dark at the end of the drive.

"I'll wait here," Randy said when he pulled the taxi to a stop.

Abraham helped Julia from the car. Together they walked to the porch where Abraham rapped gently on the door.

When no one answered, he peered through a window.

"Do you see anyone?" Julia asked.

"Sarah is probably sleeping upstairs with her daughter and Kayla." He knocked harder, and when that failed to summon anyone, he rapped again.

Julia turned to glance over her shoulder, her heart pounding. "Why doesn't Sarah answer the door?"

He shook his head and tried knocking again.

"Tell me everything is okay, Abraham, and that Mateo and Pablo haven't been here."

"Just as you mentioned, Julia. Everything is fine. We have to be patient."

"Patient? I'm scared."

"I will check the barn and see whether the buggy is there."

"Would she have taken Kayla with her?"

"She would not have left the child here alone."

Tears burned Julia's eyes. She thought of everything that had happened. Now Sarah and Kayla were gone. How could anything worse happen?

After checking the barn, Abraham hurried back to the car where Julia stood waiting. "Something must have happened," he told her. "Sarah's buggy is gone. Perhaps she needed to visit an aging relative and took Kayla and her daughter with her. She would have left a note on the door of my house with information about their whereabouts."

"If only that could be, Abraham."

Julia climbed back into the rear seat. Her heart pounded. William was still asleep, oblivious to what was happening. She had worried about him so much while they were in the city, but she never thought anything untoward would happen to Kayla. Her mistake.

She had made so many.

Why had she left Kayla with a woman she didn't even know? In hindsight, she should have taken Kayla with them to look for William. Then she thought about grabbing William in the fast food restaurant and running from Pablo and Mateo, and the unfriendly clerk at the hotel. Kayla would have gotten too tired and too frightened, plus she would have slowed them down.

No, Julia had been right to leave Kayla. But where was her daughter now?

Oh, Lord, please. I feel overwhelmed by what has hap-

pened and so very fearful. I am trying to trust, which is what I believe You want me to do, but I'm shaking inside.

If anything happened to Kayla…

She looked at Abraham. He had lost his four-year-old daughter and his wife. How had he survived all that pain?

She didn't want to be strong like he had been. She wanted to burst into tears and rail at God for putting her child in danger, although she only had herself to blame.

A hole formed in her heart and the pain of what might have happened was so powerful, she could hardly breathe.

Abraham wrapped his arm about her shoulders.

"Hurry, Randy. Take us to my farm. Sarah was not at her house. I am hopeful she left a message on my door."

Randy must have heard the fear in Abraham's voice. He turned sharply out of Sarah's property and accelerated. At this time of night, they were the only car on the country road. Darkness surrounded them, as dark as Julia's heart that was ready to break.

"Do not think of what might have happened until we have more information," Abraham said, his voice filled with compassion.

He must have known what she was thinking and that made Julia even more afraid. She could not answer him for fear her voice would turn into a scream from her heart.

The farm appeared. Randy turned the car into the drive and pulled to a stop in front of Abraham's house.

Abraham jumped out, ran up the stairs and unlocked the door. He lit an oil lamp and returned to look for a note left by the door.

Then he glanced at the taxi, his face fearful and illuminated by the flickering light. There was no note and no information about Kayla or where Sarah had taken her.

Julia climbed from the car, tears streaming from her

eyes. Her life as she knew it was about to change forever and she couldn't go on.

"Oh, Abraham." She fell into his arms and sobbed.

"Kayla is all right," he assured her.

"I don't believe you." She gasped. "Where's my baby girl?"

Abraham rubbed her shoulders. "We will find her."

"First William and now Kayla. When will it end?"

"Julia."

Hearing her name, she turned to find Sarah running toward them from the *dawdy* house.

"Where's Kayla?"

"Asleep in her room," Sarah said as she neared. "She was upset you were not home. Some of my relatives stayed at Abraham's spare house when my husband died. I still have the key, so we came here to bring comfort to Kayla. My daughter, Ella, is asleep in the bed with her. I stayed downstairs, hoping to hear you return."

Julia ran past Sarah to the porch of the *dawdy* house. She pushed open the kitchen door and took the stairs two at a time. Opening the bedroom door, she gasped with relief when she saw Kayla sleeping peacefully in her own bed. Julia dropped to her knees, tears of relief falling from her eyes. She brushed the hair off her daughter's face and kissed her cheek. Sarah's daughter was sleeping next to her, both girls oblivious to the fear and terrible thoughts that had rumbled through Julia's mind.

She stumbled into the hallway so her sobs of relief wouldn't wake the girls. Suddenly Abraham was there again, pulling her into his arms, the smell of him so masculine and strong. She never wanted to leave him.

Kayla had not been hurt or captured or harmed in any way. William was asleep in the taxi downstairs. The two Philadores were still in Kansas City, or perhaps they were already on their way back to Philadelphia. Her ex-husband was behind bars where he couldn't hurt them and she wasn't alone. She had a wonderful man who was strong and honest and understanding, who didn't laugh at her for getting upset or for fearing the worst. A man who had lost everything he had ever loved, but who still was able to open his heart to her.

"I'm sorry I got so carried away. I…I thought…"

"I know, Julia. You have had so much happen recently and you have been so strong. But everything is going to be okay. I will not let anything happened to you or to the children."

She could hear his heart beat as he held her tight, her head on his chest. Her sobs subsided, and her thoughts turned from her children, who she knew were safe, to Abraham, the man who was very much present with her now.

He pulled back ever so slightly and stared down at her. Everything stopped for one long moment, even her heart that had pounded so hard just moments earlier. The whole world seemed to be on pause as she looked into his eyes. His lips twitched, as if he didn't know whether or not he should draw her closer. All she wanted was for him to lower his lips to hers. Although she didn't know if she could survive if he did.

"Julia." He whispered her name, yet so much more was contained in that one word than she had ever heard from anyone.

She stretched toward him, wanting nothing to keep them apart. All she wanted was for his mouth to touch hers.

Her heart pounded in anticipation. She reached her hands around his neck and buried her fingers in his hair as his lips slowly descended to—

"Abraham?"

Sarah was on the stairs, calling up to them.

He pulled back, startled.

Julia's heart stopped, this time with regret.

She backed away, unable to speak, feeling drained and tired. Her mind swirled with confusion wondering how she had gone from tears of fear to a yearning to remain in this man's arms forever.

"I need to bring William inside." She pushed past Abraham and hurried down the stairs, her hand gripping the railing lest she lose her balance. She felt weak and confused.

"Is everything all right?" Sarah asked as Julia hurried toward the kitchen door.

"Yes. Thank you for caring for Kayla. She's sound asleep. I need to bring William inside."

"I am sorry to have frightened you when you found no one home at my house," Sarah said, following her.

Julia turned and took the woman's hand. "You have been so gracious, and I am grateful. But today has been long and troubling. That everything turned out all right brings me comfort. Your friendship and help does, as well, Sarah. Please let me know how I can repay you for your kindness."

The Amish woman smiled. "No payment is needed. You would help me in the same way if I had a need."

Julia nodded. "That's true."

Abraham came down the stairs. "I must pay Randy." He looked at Sarah. "Would you like to stay the night here?"

She shook her head. "Ella and I should get home. Would you hitch my horse to the buggy?"

"Of course, it is not a problem. I will ask Randy to follow your buggy to ensure you and Ella arrive home safely."

Julia helped her sleepy son from the car and guided him upstairs to bed. By the time she left his room, Sarah's horse and buggy were waiting in the driveway. Her daughter slipped easily from bed and smiled sweetly as she and her mother left the *dawdy* house to return home.

Once they had driven off, followed by the Amish taxi, Abraham stepped back into the kitchen. He looked expectantly at Julia, as if he wanted to take her in his arms again, but the moment had passed and she had returned to her senses.

She was grateful to Abraham, and he was a man who made her think of being open to love again, although that still seemed almost impossible. She would never be able to trust anyone with her heart, even an Amish man who had saved her son.

The realization that she would go through life alone brought a sense of sorrow again.

But she had her children. What more could she want?

As Abraham left the house and she closed and locked the door behind him, Julia realized that she did want something more. She wanted someone like Abraham to be a part of her life.

But that could never be, and that thought brought tears to her eyes as she climbed the stairs and slipped into her bedroom.

Tomorrow would be a new day. Everything would look brighter in the sunlight. She would be rid of foolish thoughts about love and happiness, things she wanted but would never have.

FOURTEEN

Abraham headed to the barn early the next morning to catch up on the chores that had not been done while he was gone. He had moved the horses to the pasture so they could graze and get water from the pond and they had fared well, but a farm took work, as he had told Julia the first morning she was here, and there was much to do.

He tried to focus on his labor, but he kept thinking of when she had been in his arms and the way she had felt so soft and warm and inviting. More than anything he had wanted to kiss her. Then Sarah had called out to them.

Too quickly, Julia had pulled free from his embrace, which left him feeling empty and flummoxed by all that had happened. Today he would behave more appropriately and stay more aloof. Clearly that was what Julia wanted, judging by the way she had rushed away from him.

He stopped for a minute and peered out the open door of the barn toward the house where she and her children slept. He would not wake them for breakfast this morning. They needed to sleep.

Just as long as Julia did not hole up inside the house and ignore him. He could not endure that, yet that might occur and if so, he would handle it as best he could.

The day was overcast and fit his mood. He should be giving thanks for their success in finding William and bringing him back home. Abraham was grateful, and he knew too well how things could have turned out, especially with two opposing gangs up in arms.

He had filled the troughs with water and mangers with feed, spread hay for the cattle and mended a broken patch of fencing before anyone stirred in the *dawdy* house.

A door slammed and he turned to see William dressed in Amish clothing heading toward him. The boy still looked tired, but he nodded a greeting and reached for a shovel that rested against the side of the barn.

"I'll muck out the stalls," the boy stated without preamble.

"How are you today, William?"

The boy shrugged. "I am glad to be here."

"Your clothes look good on you. Was it a problem to dress?"

"*Mamm* helped me hook the suspenders."

Mamm? He had used the Pennsylvania Dutch term for mother.

"Your mother is up?" Abraham asked, hoping the feelings he had for Julia were not evident in his tone.

"She is making breakfast. Kayla is helping her. She said she will ring the dinner bell when the food is ready."

"You are hungry, I am sure."

The boy smiled. "I am very hungry, but we will work first and then eat."

Abraham nodded, grateful to hear a new energy in William's voice. Much had happened to him on his trip to Kansas City, probably more than the boy realized. He had left Yoder in the middle of the night as a youth yearning to join a gang of street thugs, and in less than twenty-four hours he had turned into a level-headed young man. It was almost too much to believe could be true.

"*Danke*, *Gott*," Abraham said under his breath.

Within the hour, the door of the *dawdy* house opened and Kayla rang the dinner bell.

"Your mother has timed breakfast perfectly," he told William. "We have finished the morning chores. After we eat, we will check on Mr. Raber's animals."

"And the phone to see if any calls have come through?"

"We will certainly do that." Abraham pointed to the corner of the barn. "Leave the shovel. We must wash up at the pump and then enjoy the food your mother has prepared."

The water from the pump was cold. Abraham handed William the bar of soap and watched with approval as the boy rolled up his sleeves and scrubbed his arms up to his elbows in the chilly water to ensure the muck from the barn did not come with them to the dining table. Once they had washed, they dried their hands and arms on the towel that hung near the pump and headed to the house. Abraham wiped his boots on the rug by the door and smiled when William did the same.

Opening the door, Abraham was pleasantly accosted by the hearty smell of coffee, and bacon and eggs, and biscuits, hot from the oven. He stepped inside and searched for Julia, but the kitchen was empty.

"*Mamm*?" William called.

She came running down the stairs, looking bright-eyed and beautiful. Abraham's breath hitched, and he was taken aback by the flush in her cheeks and the twinkle in her eyes. She had pulled her hair into a bun at the base of her neck and had settled the *kapp* on her head, the strings hanging loose at her neck along with a long strand of hair that had either pulled free or had escaped capture when she first fixed her hair.

She straightened her apron and smiled in welcome. "You are hungry, I'm sure."

Abraham nodded. "The kitchen is filled with wonderful smells. You have been working hard to provide a hearty breakfast, for which I am grateful, Julia."

"It is the least I can do after what you have done for us, Abraham. Sit at the table and I will pour coffee and then fix the plates."

She brought a filled mug to the table. Her coffee tasted far better than the bitter brew he sometimes made. "Good coffee," he said with gratitude.

"I'm still not used to boiling water and pouring it over the grounds in the drip coffee pot. I tried to keep it hot on the back burner but fear the heat was too high. I am glad it meets your approval."

Kayla raced downstairs and ran to Abraham with her arms open wide. He had not expected her exuberant hello or the warm hugs she gave him. "You were gone so long," the child said. "I was worried."

"But you were okay staying with Sarah and her daughter."

"Yes, but I wanted to be here at your house so I could see you as soon as you returned. That's why Miss Sarah brought me here to sleep last night. When I woke this morning, I saw *Mamm* smiling down at me."

Kayla's statement that she had wanted to be at his house touched Abraham, as well as her waking to find Julia.

Noting her empty arms, Abraham asked, "Where is your doll?"

"Ella said Amish girls don't play with dolls because they are busy helping their mothers with their own sisters and brothers."

"That does not mean you cannot play with your doll."

"Annie is resting. She didn't sleep well last night."

"You are still calling her Annie?" he asked.

"*Yah.*"

He smiled as she used the Amish word for *yes*.

"*Yah*," Kayla repeated. "Annie is her name. We have all changed and you said you would call her Annie, so I will, too. It is a *gut* name, *yah*?"

"For sure, Kayla." He chuckled. "It is a *gut* name."

"Ella said that Amish girls my age cook and do housework."

He winked. "They also find time to play. You have years to work. Plus, now you must do your studies."

"Kayla, you are full of energy this morning," Julia called from the stove. "Come and take this plate to Abraham."

The plate was heaped high with food, and Kayla set it on the table in front of him.

William slipped onto the bench after he poured milk for Kayla and himself.

"*Danke*," he said when Kayla brought his plate to the table.

She took her own plate from her mother and sat next to her brother.

Julia checked the stove and then stepped to the table. Abraham stood and helped her with her chair.

William stood, too.

Kayla smiled. "William, tomorrow you can help me with my chair."

The boy laughed and then returned to the bench.

"The food looks delicious. Let us give thanks." Abraham bowed his head, but before he could offer a silent prayer, Kayla nudged him. "Why don't you pray out loud and then we can all pray together."

He glanced at Julia, who looked expectantly back at him.

Kayla wrinkled her brow. "Miss Sarah said praying

out loud is not the Amish way, but maybe just this once we could, please, Abraham?"

"That would be nice, Kayla." He held out his hand to the child. She took his and William's. The boy reached for one of Julia's hands, and Abraham held the other.

Warm contentment swept over him as he bowed his head. "Thank you, *Gott*, for bringing us together and for keeping us safe. We give You thanks for this food and for all who worked to provide this meal. May it nourish us so we can do the work You have called us to do. Amen."

The others intoned *amen* and without taking a breath, the children reached for their forks and started eating.

Abraham smiled at Julia. "Thank you for preparing such a delicious breakfast for us, Julia."

"You're most welcome, Abraham. Thank you for providing this nice house in which to stay."

"I hope we stay here forever," Kayla said as she swallowed a forkful of egg and then reached for her glass of milk.

"Abraham does not need us underfoot that long, Kayla," Julia said.

Her words brought Abraham back to the reality of their situation. Just as Julia mentioned, she and the children would eventually move on to another location and another identity once the danger eased. He doubted Jonathan wanted them to stay here indefinitely. Still, it was something he might mention to his friend.

"I need to call Jonathan and check on a few things with him. William and I will tend to the farm across the way and then we can all go to town so I can make the phone call. We will also stop at the grocery for supplies."

"Ice cream, too?" Kayla asked.

"We will see about the ice cream, Kayla."

"Are you sure we should go into town?" Julia asked. "Can't you use your neighbor's phone?"

"I could, but it might be smarter to use a pay phone, in case anyone is tracking Mr. Raber's number. Using a pay phone in town will be an added precaution."

Julia's face clouded.

"Do not worry," he assured her. "Besides, a trip to town will be enjoyable."

"What if it rains?" Kayla asked.

Abraham glanced out the window. "It is cloudy, but I do not think we will have rain. Are you made of sugar?" he teased.

"Sugar?"

"I thought all little girls were sweet as sugar."

She giggled. "No, Mr. Abraham. I am not made of sugar. I am made of flesh and blood."

"And you are smart, too. You take after your mother."

Kayla grinned and looked at Julia. "Then William takes after our father."

"I do not," the boy insisted.

"Do too," Kayla replied. "You're a boy. That means you take after him."

"Enough, Kayla," Julia said. "You are each unique and special. Is that understood?"

"Still—"

Julia tilted her head. "It's time to eat instead of talk, young lady."

The child sighed with exasperation. Abraham squelched a smile. Kayla was precocious, which was cute at this age. Just as long as she learned how to temper her remarks as she aged.

He glanced at William with his downcast eyes and flushed face. Kayla's comment seemed to have cut William to the quick.

"The chores in the barn were done more quickly today because William helped me." The boy glanced up. Abraham nodded his appreciation. "You have a fine worker in your son, Julia. I know you are proud of him."

She smiled. "I'm glad you recognize his willingness to serve, Abraham. Both my children are eager to help whenever they can."

Kayla's eyes widened as she accepted her mother's praise and seemed less interested in her brother and more in her breakfast.

Children made life interesting and challenging, but also filled it with joy and love. Abraham thought of his Becca with her big blue eyes and curly blond hair. The pain was real as he thought of all he had lost.

"You look sad, Mr. Abraham."

Kayla was staring at him, her eyes wide. The concern he read in her sweet gaze was like salve to his wounded heart.

He forced a smile, not wanting to pull Julia or her children into his own sorrow. "I am fine, Kayla, but food remains on your plate. You need to eat now so you can go with us to town."

"Will we stop at the store where we bought our *kapps*?"

He glanced at Julia. "Is there something you need?"

"I need nothing." She turned to her daughter. "Is there some reason you wanted to return to the store?"

"I wanted to get another *kapp* in case I lose this one. Ella said they get dirty when we play outside and sometimes the wind pulls them off our heads and into the air." She touched her *kapp*. "I do not want to lose mine, but it might happen."

"If so, we will get another one then, Kayla. For now, just be careful when you go outside to play."

"Did you enjoy Sarah's daughter?" Abraham asked.

"Ella's nice. I helped her do her chores. After that, we played tag. Miss Sarah said I will need a larger dress soon, and if so, she has one that her daughter can no longer wear."

"Miss Sarah is very thoughtful," Julia said.

"She also will get some clothes for William."

"I don't need more clothing," he insisted.

Julia looked sharply at her son. "We will be grateful for anything Miss Sarah provides. Isn't that right, William?"

He shrugged. "I guess so. Maybe she will bake another pie." The boy glanced at his mother and widened his eyes. "Mom, you used to bake. A cherry pie would be good."

"With ice cream," Kayla added.

Julia laughed. "We can look for canned cherries at the grocery store."

"Yum." Kayla smiled as she scooped the last of her eggs into her mouth.

Once everyone had eaten, Julia stood and began to clear the table. "If you would like more coffee, Abraham…"

He held up his hand. "I have had enough. William and I will go to my neighbor's farm. When we return, we will prepare for our trip to town."

"Yay!"

"Finish your milk, Kayla, and help clear the table."

"Yes, *Mamm*."

Abraham smiled. Julia did, as well. If only children could remain innocent longer, he thought.

He glanced back and waited as William drank the last of his milk. The boy carried his plate and glass to the sink, rinsed the dishes and placed them on the counter.

"See you soon," Julia said as she carted another plate to the sink.

Abraham put his hand on the boy's shoulder as they

walked outside. The pain he had felt earlier eased and was replaced with a sense of well-being.

Working together, they fed and watered the livestock at the neighbor's house. On the way back, they stopped at the phone shack. William stayed outside as Abraham checked the answering machine. The one voicemail was from a telemarketer.

After deleting the message, Abraham stepped from the shack. "Let us go home, William. You can help me harness Buttercup for our trip to town."

The boy nodded, then he glanced again at the phone shack. "Were there any messages?"

"Are you expecting a phone call?" Abraham asked.

William shook his head and hung his head. "No, but I thought David might call since I never met up with his brother."

"Maybe David realizes being in the gang is not a good thing."

"Maybe. David's mother never wanted him to get involved with anything Pablo did. She said someday they would leave the city and go to live with her sister in the country."

"What did David think about that?"

William shrugged. "He said the country might be nice, especially if he could be outside more and if there were animals to play with. He always wanted a dog."

"What about you, William?"

"I wanted a dog, too, but now I would tell him about Buttercup and the other horses and cows, and what I've learned to do."

"You have learned much because you are a good listener."

"That's what Mrs. Fielding said. Kayla talks a lot, but I talk when I have something important to say."

Abraham put his hand on the boy's back as they walked back to the farm. "You are becoming very wise, William."

The boy smiled and nodded as if he thought the same thing.

William seemed to have learned the importance of having a home and a mother who loved him. If only he could have felt love from his father, too. Maybe the pain of that loss would ease with time. Until then, Abraham would try to offer good advice for as long as William and his mother stayed with him.

Right now, he wished they would stay for a very long time.

FIFTEEN

The wind had picked up, and Julia held on to her *kapp* as the buggy headed toward town.

"Perhaps Kayla was right," she said to Abraham. "I may need to get a second *kapp* in case this one blows away in the wind."

He looked at the sky. "The strong wind brings a chill to the air. You and the children might want to cover your legs with blankets. They are behind the last seat."

Without being told, William stretched back and retrieved two blankets. He handed one to his mother and the other to Kayla.

Julia helped her daughter arrange the covering over her legs. "William, do you want to cover your legs?"

"I'm not cold," he said.

Julia enjoyed the warmth of the blanket and draped part of it over Abraham's legs.

He smiled at her and nodded. "You are very thoughtful, but I am not cold. We will be in town soon."

"The wind is brisk, Abraham. You do not want to get sick."

"I am more concerned about you and Kayla." He glanced over his shoulder at her son. "William and I will be fine."

"*Yah*," the boy answered with his new attempt at using Pennsylvania Dutch. "Abraham taught me a few phrases when we were working in the barn. *Es ist heute nicht so kalt*."

Julia lifted her brow. "Would someone translate?"

Abraham laughed. "William said it is not so cold today in German. Meaning we do not need the blanket."

"What about Pennsylvania Dutch?"

Abraham nodded. "We will work on that soon."

"Someday I will need to learn the Amish language if I want to understand my own son."

William patted her shoulder. "Don't worry, *Mamm*. I will always tell you what I'm saying."

She grabbed his hand and felt a swell of gratitude.

"When will we be in town?" Kayla asked.

"Soon, Kayla."

"Do I need an Amish first name?" the child asked.

"Your name is Kayla," Julia said. "It's a lovely name and suits you well. We'll stick with that one."

"You and William will keep your names, too?" the child asked.

"Don't talk about new names," her brother warned. "You never know who will hear you."

"You called Davey Davila," she said with a huff.

"I made a mistake, okay? We move on when we make a mistake. That's what Abraham told me. We don't look to the past. We look to the future."

Julia reached for Abraham's hand and squeezed it. William had been listening. Whether their Amish protector realized it or not, her son was drawn to Abraham and wanted to do what was right in his eyes. His own father had never given him attention, and the boy hungered for male guidance. Julia could only do so much. Abraham was a good role model for William. If only they could remain with him a bit longer.

Given the opportunity to talk to Jonathan privately, she would ask if they could stay in Yoder. The children were taking to the Amish way of life, and they both liked Abraham. Neither child needed another change in their lives. Julia didn't want to change locations, either. She liked the farm, but she liked Abraham even more. He was a good influence on her children. He was a good influence on her, as well.

Riding to town with Julia at his side and the children in the rear of the buggy made Abraham all the more aware of his feelings for Julia and her family. He glanced at her, seeing her flushed cheeks and warm smile. She took in the surrounding area with the Amish farms and neighbors, some of whom had reached out to Abraham when he first arrived. He had appreciated their welcome and willingness to help if and when he needed extra hands to harvest or bale hay or any of the other jobs a farm demanded. Regrettably, he had remained somewhat aloof and kept to himself far too much.

Julia with her sweet disposition would fit in well with the women in the area. Never once had he heard her complain about the lack of worldly items. She had cooked on the wood-burning stove, made delicious coffee and even baked biscuits that were light and fluffy and so different from the overcooked and flavorless lumps of flour he pulled from the oven.

He glanced over his shoulder at the children who seemed lost in their own thoughts. The breeze blew their hair back from their sweet faces and their contented smiles brought a warmth to Abraham's heart that filled him with joy.

Even Julia seemed more lighthearted today, as if the struggle of the past was over and a new time of peace and happiness appeared on the horizon.

Abraham wanted to fully embrace that new dawn, but he had to be practical. The Philadores were tough adversaries, and until he knew otherwise, Abraham would keep up his guard.

"The grocery downtown has a pay phone," he shared. "We will shop and then call Jonathan."

Julia leaned closer. "But will he know anything about Pablo and his friend?"

"The marshals have informants. We should be able to learn what the Philadores are planning."

"I pray they are planning to stay in Philadelphia and have abandoned any desire to find William."

"You are in danger, too, Julia. You saw the men who broke into your apartment. Plus, you saw Pablo in Kansas City and could incriminate all of them."

"We will trust the gang is concerned about other issues, do you not agree?"

Her smile lit up her face. "I agree. We must trust."

If only Julia could trust him. He had not been able to protect his wife and child. He could not become complacent and make a similar mistake again.

He jiggled the reins to hurry Buttercup along and glanced at the oncoming traffic. Any car passing by could be a threat. He did not want to live his life in fear, but he needed to be cautious and on guard.

"I made a list of some of the things we'll need at the grocery." Julia opened the tote she had placed at her feet in the buggy and pulled out a sheet of paper. "Will the store be different than the groceries I'm used to?"

"More items are sold in bulk. Anything dry, such as

flour and corn starch and spices—even powdered laundry detergent—is packaged in plastic bags."

"So I won't find the brands I'm used to?"

"I am sure many of the products you bought in Pennsylvania will be available for purchase. After all, the grocery serves the *Englisch* community in addition to the *Amish.* Although the selection may be more limited."

"What about the meat?"

"The meat market has a butcher. He makes sausage and provides other selections typical to the Amish." He chuckled. "Do you like pig's feet?"

She rolled her eyes. "Tell me it's a Pennsylvania Dutch delicacy."

"Some like it. My mother served it with homemade noodles over mashed potatoes and gravy."

"Noodles and potatoes are eaten together?"

He laughed at the surprised look on her face. "A lot of carbohydrates, but so good. Sarah can teach you to make the noodles."

"She's already done so much. I need an Amish cookbook."

"Perhaps we can find this at the store, as well."

"Is there something I could give Sarah as a thank-you for keeping Kayla?"

"She does not expect a gift for being a good neighbor."

"Still..." Julia thought for a moment. "I want her to know how grateful I am."

"Before you and the children arrived, Sarah had asked me to help her at the upcoming flea market in Yoder. I planned to sell some of my neighbor's furniture for him if he does not return home before then. Sarah will have a table nearby and sell her quilts and other handmade items."

"We could help her that day."

"First we will see what Jonathan has to say. If the Philadores have eased their search for William, we can attend the flea market. Otherwise, we will stay home and out of sight until all of this is over."

"Will that time ever come, Abraham?"

"I pray it will be over soon."

If the Philadores ended their search for William, the marshals might move the family to a less isolated area and back into the *Englisch* world.

Saying goodbye to the children would be hard. Saying goodbye to Julia would be even more difficult.

SIXTEEN

Julia enjoyed visiting the grocery and felt like a child in a toy store at Christmas. As Abraham had mentioned, many of the products she used in Pennsylvania were available for purchase. She placed a number of items in her cart, including canned cherries for the pie she would bake sometime soon.

The dry items, sold in bulk, intrigued her. Powdered chicken stock for soups, flour and sugar, corn starch and a myriad of spices, including pickling spices that she had never used. Just as Abraham had mentioned, they were packaged in clear cellophane bags with a store label.

"I'll need to ask Sarah about canning," she said to Abraham as she browsed the shelves.

"There is time," he assured her. "First we must plant the fields and grow the crops before harvest."

"I have a feeling I'll be busy throughout the summer."

If Jonathan would allow them to stay with Abraham that long. She would talk to him today about her preferences.

The children had noticed the small lunch area at the front of the store when they entered. Kayla kept mentioning that ice cream was sold by the cone—and candy by the pound.

"We'll shop first," Julia said.

They passed another Amish family and Kayla, always the extrovert, waved at the little girl and smiled at the mother.

"We like this store," Kayla announced to the woman.

"You are new to Yoder?" the Amish shopper asked, eying both of them.

Julia groaned inwardly. She should have instructed Kayla not to initiate conversations, especially with adults. The Amish embraced the adage that children should be seen and not heard.

If only Abraham had been nearby to offer a response, but he and William were in the hardware section, examining nuts and bolts and screws. When had her son started appreciating anything to do with carpentry? Probably since he started hanging around their Amish host.

"We have not lived in Yoder long," Kayla responded while Julia debated whether to nod and hurry on to the next aisle or offer some type of noncommittal reply.

"My daughter never met a stranger," Julia finally said with a stilted laugh. If only the woman would continue shopping without additional comments.

"I have not seen you in town. You are living in the surrounding area?"

"In Mr. Abraham's daddy's house," Kayla explained before Julia could grab her hand and tug her to the far side of the shopping buggy.

"The *dawdy* house," Julia corrected.

"You are his sister?" the woman asked.

Julia shook her head. "Not family. I'm..."

Why was it so hard to provide the story Jonathan had told her to use? "I am the housekeeper. He lives alone and has a large farm. He needed someone to cook and clean."

The woman raised a brow. “You have known him before?”

Kayla opened her mouth as if ready to answer.

“Do you know his sister?” Julia asked the woman.

“She does not live in Yoder so I have not met her. I believe her name is Susan.”

Julia smiled. “Susan knew her brother needed domestic help.”

The woman nodded, satisfied with an explanation that Julia hadn’t actually provided.

“Enjoy your shopping.” Julia pushed the buggy and pulled Kayla along behind her. They did not stop until they had rounded the corner and were headed to a far aisle.

“Do you know Mr. Abraham’s sister, Mama?”

“I didn’t say I did, Kayla.”

“The woman thought you knew her.”

“We will let that woman think what she would like to think. Next time, I do not want you providing information to strangers. We have talked about this before.”

Kayla looked at the floor, her bottom lip coming out in a half pout, half cry that stabbed Julia’s heart. She hated that her overly friendly daughter had to be reined in like Abraham’s horse.

“In Philadelphia, you told me not to talk to strangers,” the child said. “I thought it was okay here, especially if they were Amish.”

“Strangers can wear any type of clothing, Kayla. I do not want you to be unduly frightened, but you need to be able to trust someone before you engage in a conversation. Do you understand?”

“Do you trust Mr. Abraham?”

“Why do you ask?”

“Because you started talking to him and let me talk to him right from the first morning we met.”

"Mr. Jonathan had told me about Mr. Abraham so I knew he was a good man."

"But did you trust him?"

Did she trust him now?

"I trust him enough to talk openly to him, Kayla, and you can, as well."

"What about Miss Sarah? You must trust her, since you let her take care of me while you and Mr. Abraham were trying to find William."

Circumstances had made it necessary to leave Kayla with a woman Julia had only just met. Did she trust Sarah? The question was difficult.

"Miss Sarah seems very kind. She's Abraham's friend, and he said she is to be trusted. Still, she does not need to know everything about us." Julia stared down at her daughter. "You didn't tell her about witness protection, did you?"

"I did not." Kayla made a cross on her chest. "Cross my heart."

"Do you know who I trust?" Julia asked. She put her arm around Kayla's shoulder. "I trust you. And I love you very much."

"I love you, Mama." Kayla thought for a moment and then added, "I love William, too. And Mr. Abraham."

"Did I hear my name?" Abraham and William turned the corner and stood in front of them.

"We were talking about loving you, Mr. Abraham."

His face brightened. He looked at Julia with expectation. "Such a nice thing to be discussing in the grocery. I am happy to know that I am loved."

"It was Kayla." Julia tried to backtrack. "She said she likes you very much."

"I believe the word she used was love," Abraham

teased. He appeared to be enjoying Julia's embarrassed discomfort.

"The word love has a number of meanings," Julia informed him.

"Hmmm?" He tugged on his jaw. "I thought love was love."

"No, it's not. You can love ice cream or you can love a child." She pointed to the ice cream area near the restaurant and then at both the children.

"Or you can love a woman," Abraham added, "because she brings joy to your life and makes you a better man."

Julia's heart thumped. Her cheeks burned. Abraham stared into her eyes and wouldn't avert his glance. Everything around them faded, and all she could focus on was the intriguing half smile that curved his lips, the lips she had wanted to kiss last night.

"Did you say ice cream, Mr. Abraham?" Kayla tugged on his hand.

The spell was broken. He glanced at the child. "What is your favorite flavor?"

"Guess," she said.

"Chocolate."

Kayla giggled. "Mama told you, right?"

"Your mother and I have never discussed ice cream, but I know what little girls like."

"Do you know William's favorite flavor?"

Abraham thought for a moment and then raised a brow. "Mint chocolate chip when available, otherwise strawberry."

Kayla's mouth dropped open. "You know everything, Mr. Abraham."

"I know when it is time to check out so we can get ice cream cones for two very special children."

He turned to Julia. "Have you finished shopping?"

"I still need a cookbook."

"The next aisle over. The children and I will take the shopping cart to the checkout stand and meet you there."

"I'll stay with *Mamm*," William said. Julia had a feeling he thought she needed someone to protect her in case there was a problem.

"We won't be long," she assured Abraham.

They found the book section and she quickly decided on a cookbook.

"*Mamm*." William lowered his voice. "Abraham and I talked about ice cream before we saw you and Kayla. That's how he knew my favorite flavors."

"I thought as much. Kayla will find out soon enough, but right now she is impressed with Abraham's uncanny knowledge. Letting her believe a bit longer isn't a bad thing, William, and knowing Kayla, she will probably come to that conclusion on her own."

"She told me she wants to call him *datt*."

Julia stared at her son, perplexed. "What does she want to call him?"

"*Datt*," William repeated. "The Pennsylvania Dutch word for dad."

"She struggles to remember your father," Julia said. "She was barely five when he left."

"I remember him."

From the look on her son's face, Julia knew the memories weren't good. "Your father loved you, William, even though he did not know how to show that love."

"I would rather he loved me less and showed it more."

"Of course you do. My own father did not show his love so I had to trust my instincts. He was my father, therefore he loved me."

"I can't do that. I know he was my father, but too much happened. I can't trust him and I can't love him."

"I wish my love was enough for you, William."

"Aw, Mom, it is enough. It's just that I would also like to feel loved by my father."

"Maybe someday."

William shook his head. "It's too late." He motioned her to follow him. "Let's go to the cash register. Then maybe we can buy ice cream."

Ice cream might smooth over a little irritation, but not the deep-seated feeling of being abandoned and unloved. Julia had struggled with both throughout her life. She hated that William had the same feelings of unworthiness.

They walked together to the checkout counter. Kayla was helping Abraham take the items from the shopping basket and place them on the conveyer belt. Kayla laughed while Abraham smiled at her with a look that Julia would have loved to have seen on her own father's face. Abraham was providing what both children needed, a strong bond with a good man who seemed to care deeply about their well-being, and for that, Julia was grateful.

"We would like two double-dip ice cream cones," Abraham said to the lady scooping up ice cream. "Chocolate and mint chocolate chip."

He looked at the children. "Waffle or cake cones?"

"Waffle," they both answered in unison.

"What about you, Julia? Surely you would enjoy an ice cream cone."

She laughed. "One scoop of butter pecan, if they have it."

He glanced at the flavors. "They do, but make that a double."

"And you, sir?" the lady asked as she handed the cones to the children.

"Not today." He paid for the cones and then headed everyone outside where they loaded the groceries onto the buggy. "You children stay here and eat your ice cream. Your mother and I need to make a phone call."

"May we sit in the buggy?" William asked.

"Of course. We will be on the phone just inside the grocery if you need anything."

Abraham lifted Kayla into the buggy and placed her on the front seat. William crawled in next to her.

"I'll play like I'm driving," the boy said as he licked his cone.

"Before long you will know how to handle the buggy, William. Plus, Buttercup takes to you. Be patient now and all that you wish will come to be soon enough."

He and Julia walked back inside to place the call.

Jonathan answered on the second ring. "I was just thinking of you, Abraham, my friend."

"I hope good thoughts. We came to town to use a pay phone in case Pablo's brother has given my neighbor's number to the Philadores."

"You no longer need to worry. The gang is focused on other issues. We have had no mention of their search for William in the last twenty-four hours."

"I am not sure that means anything."

"It will when I tell you what we learned from Kansas City."

Abraham pushed the receiver closer to his ear.

"Pablo Davila," Jonathan continued, "and his friend, Mateo Gonzales, were killed in the gunfire that erupted the night you were in the city."

"Both men are dead?"

"That's it exactly. The police haven't confirmed the details, but our sources are reliable. Plus, there's an added bit of information that's come out of the shootout."

"Tell me the Philadores have all been arrested, and I will be very happy."

"If only. That's what I dream about at night."

"I thought you would dream about your pretty wife and the children you will have someday."

Jonathan chuckled. "Actually, Celeste is pregnant."

"Congrats, buddy. You will make a great dad."

"I appreciate the vote of confidence." Jonathan hesitated before adding, "Here's what we've learned about the Kansas City street fight. The word is that a young kid was killed in the shootings. Some sources say the kid is William."

"I am confused."

"And rightfully so. For whatever reason, the word from Kansas City is that Pablo and Mateo were gunned down. A young teen who was with them died, as well. The name I hear is William Bradford."

"William is outside, waiting in the buggy."

"But our informants claim he was killed. The Philadores called off the search for William because they believe he died in the crossfire. I hate that anyone had to die, but having them call off their search plays into our hands perfectly."

"So someone else's loss is good news for us?"

"We're not even sure a teen died, Abraham. Rumors can start that are completely unfounded. We'll learn more as time passes. But you can all breathe a little more easily. Tell Julia."

"She is here with me and wants to talk to you."

"Great. Before you put her on, I just wanted to say thank you, Abraham. You've done an outstanding job keeping the family safe. I told you William would be a problem."

"The issue has turned around," Abraham assured him.

"Only because of your guidance, I have a feeling. I apologize about leaving you high and dry in Kansas City, but we couldn't buck Mother Nature. Who would think we'd have a snowstorm this late in the season or that it would stop everything on the East Coast? Thankfully, you handled it."

"A guy named Grant is a regular at the Fellowship Church shelter we stayed out. He was instrumental in getting us out of a very bad situation and deserves the praise. The manager of the shelter—a woman named Muriel—does, as well, if anything can be done on your end. Either a financial contribution to the shelter or connecting Grant with agencies that can help him as he reaches out to the kids on the street. They both took a liking to William and were instrumental in keeping us safe and ensuring we left the city unharmed during a very dangerous time."

"You've got me thinking, Abraham. Either of your Good Samaritans could have started that rumor about the kid's death so no one would follow you back to Yoder."

And to ensure William remained safe. Abraham nodded, realizing Jonathan might be right.

"I'll contact some folks in Kansas City," the marshal continued, "and put in a good word for both of them. We'll see what can come of it, although your name won't be mentioned."

"I do not want to be connected in any way, Jonathan. Julia and I need to remain completely out of the picture."

"I hear you and agree completely."

Abraham lowered the phone from his ear and motioned Julia closer.

"The kids are sitting in the buggy as if they're an Amish couple leaving the market," she said.

"I will check on them while you talk to Jonathan."

A smidge of ice cream hung on the edge of her upper

lip. Abraham used his thumb to lift it off. Touching her sent a jolt though his body. Their eyes connected and more was exchanged in that one glance than they had said last night at the house.

What was wrong with him? He felt like a pool of wet cement when he was around Julia, unable to get back into the form he used to be. Now all he could think about was her, and how much, even in this grocery store, he wanted to wrap her in his arms.

Abraham handed her the phone and then stepped away to keep from reaching out to her and embarrassing both of them. There was something magnetic about Julia, something that made him feel stronger and more protective when he was around her. He had never felt that way before. Perhaps it was because he knew how fleeting love could be and feared it as much as he wanted it in his life.

"Jonathan?" She raised the receiver to her ear. Her voice sounded strained as if she, too, had felt that pull between them.

Abraham needed fresh air and space away from Julia to think straight again. She and her children were with him for a limited period of time. With the Philadores no longer looking for William, the family would probably leave the Amish area and take up a new residence after William testified at the gang leader's trail. Once they left Yoder, they would never return.

They would live their new lives free of the gangs, and Abraham would be left alone to remember all the special memories and blessings they had brought to his life. He needed to remain strong. Later he would grieve their leaving, which was bound to happen. Without the children and Julia, life would not be the same. Life would never be as good as this again.

SEVENTEEN

"I'm not ready to leave Yoder," Julia said to Jonathan. She moved the receiver closer to her ear, grateful that Abraham was heading outside so she could have the chance to speak truthfully.

"I don't understand."

"I'm not sure how long you planned to leave us here, but I wanted you to know that the children have bonded with Abraham. He's had a positive influence on them and I hope you'll let us stay in Yoder."

"That's good to know, Julia. I thought Abraham would provide a welcome refuge for you and the children. Hold on a minute." Someone spoke to him before he came back on the line. "Sorry to cut our conversation short, but I need to get to a meeting. Have Abraham tell you what we learned about the Philadores."

Julia hung up and started for the door, but when she stepped outside her heart stopped, seeing the chaos that had had erupted.

Buttercup was running wild, galloping down the middle of the street, eyes wide and ears back, pulling the buggy with Julia's two children in it at breakneck speed. The buggy creaked and shimmied as if ready to snap apart.

Kayla's frantic screams filled the air. William sat in the front, ashen-faced, his hand stretched toward the dropped reins that dragged along the road. Abraham ran alongside, arms flailing to stop the runaway horse.

Julia dropped her half-eaten cone and ran after them. “God,” she cried. “Help my children.”

A car approached from the opposite direction driving much too fast. Didn’t the driver see the buggy?

“No,” Julia screamed. The car turned onto a side street and accelerated.

Abraham grabbed Buttercup’s mane and leaped onto the horse’s back. Grabbing the harness, he pulled back. “Whoa. Whoa, Buttercup. Calm down, girl. Whoa.”

The horse fought his control, but slowed and eventually came to a stop.

Julia gasped with relief and ran toward the buggy.

“Mama,” Kayla cried, her arms outstretched.

Julia pulled her daughter into her embrace and offered a hand to help William down. His palms were sweaty, his face white. He leaned into her embrace, visibly shaken.

“You’re okay,” she soothed.

Abraham slipped off Buttercup’s back and patted the horse. He reached for the reins that had fallen to the ground and guided the horse and buggy to an asphalt parking lot at the side of a nearby building. He tethered the horse to the hitching rail and continued to speak calmly to the frightened mare.

Julia, still holding Kayla in her arms, approached the buggy. William followed, his head hanging.

“What happened?” Abraham asked.

The boy said nothing.

“How did Buttercup come unhitched, William?”

“I…I was pretending to drive the buggy.”

“Which I told you we would work on at a later time. Were you holding the reins and did you encourage Buttercup forward?”

"I held the reins, but I didn't tell her to go. It was the car."

"What car?"

"It came up from behind us and swerved close. Someone threw something from the window at Buttercup. It hit her rump. That's when she spooked and started to run wild."

"You pulled back on the reins?"

"I tried. I had my ice cream and somehow the reins slipped out of my hold."

Kayla wiped her eyes and wiggled to get down. "William's right, Mr. Abraham. We were in the buggy, licking our ice cream cones, and then the car came so fast."

"What color was the car?"

"I think it was red," Kayla said.

William nodded. "It was a red sports car. The driver looked like the guy the sheriff stopped the first time we came to town. There was another man, standing on the sidewalk. I didn't see him until the buggy jerked forward. He had a camera in his hands."

Abraham studied the street. "Wait here. I want to find whatever was thrown."

"You're both all right," Julia told the children. She needed to be strong for them, but her heart was pounding so hard, thinking of what could have happened.

Abraham returned carrying an unopened beer can. "I did not see the man with the camera, but I found this on the side of the road, near where I had left the buggy."

"Who would throw a beer can at the horse?" Julia asked.

"Someone who wanted to make trouble."

Julia groaned, realizing who would have wanted to harm her children. "It was Pablo. He must have checked the bus schedule in Kansas City and realized where William's bus had originated."

Abraham motioned Julia away from the children so they

would not hear their conversation. “Jonathan assured me that Pablo and his friend were involved in the gang shooting the night we escaped. It escalated and they were killed.”

Julia gasped. “As much as I wanted Pablo stopped, I hate to think of his poor mother. Oh, Abraham, there’s been too much bloodshed.”

“The Philadores have stopped searching for William.”

“But why? Although I’m grateful.”

“Jonathan’s sources claim a teen was killed in the Kansas City shooting,” Abraham said, his voice low. “They got word that it was William. Evidently the Philadores thought Pablo had apprehended the boy and was taking him back to Philly.”

“I don’t like to hear of any child dying.”

“Neither do I, Julia. The report could be bogus. Grant and the two men who helped us could have started the rumor to ensure we eluded the gang members.”

“You think Grant would have done that?”

“If he thought William was in danger. No matter how the rumor started, I am relieved that the Philadores are no longer looking for your son.”

“I’m relieved, too,” Julia said. “But who threw the beer can?”

“The children mentioned a red sports car. It could have been the guys we saw outside Trotter’s Dry Goods. But they are not the only ones who might cause trouble.”

He shook his head with frustration. “The Amish are frequently attacked by teens or people who find our way of life strange. They try to cause problems. Amish on bicycles have been run off roads and crashed while drivers of cars laugh at the damage they cause. Some of the so-called pranks can be dangerous, if not deadly. The world does not like people who are different, Julia.”

“You can’t generalize about the world, Abraham. Some

people are intolerant. They don't have a strong moral compass and are inconsiderate of others. Those people have hate in their hearts, but that's not everyone. The world is filled with good people, I have to believe that."

She sighed, feeling sad and unsettled. "Let's go home. We have groceries to unload and dinner to cook. Perhaps on the farm we can forget what happened today. It's time to think good thoughts and to heal from the past."

"The children are upset," Abraham said, glancing at them.

"Fresh air and caring for the animals will help them see another side of life, Abraham. That will be *gut*, very, very *gut*."

He smiled and her heart skittered in her chest.

"Now you are talking like an Amish woman."

She glanced down at her long dress. "If I dress Amish, I must learn to speak Pennsylvania Dutch and embrace your culture. *Gut* is one of the few words I know, along with *danke*. Thank you, Abraham, for providing for us and for keeping us safe. You've gotten us through a hard time, but that's about to change, especially with the news Jonathan provided today. I'm relieved and rejoicing that all of the hardship is behind us." She held out her hand and took his. "Let's think of better things than hateful people, whether they are in Philadelphia or Kansas City or Yoder. Let's focus on all that is good and wholesome."

He nodded. "That sounds *gut* to me, Julia."

"*Yah*," she sighed. "That sounds *gut* to me, as well."

They climbed into the buggy and headed back to the farm. The sun peeked through the clouds and warmed them. Kayla and William were quiet but seemed to have moved past the incident at the grocery. They were ready to embrace their new life, just as Julia was.

EIGHTEEN

For the next few days, Abraham refused to think about Julia and her family leaving Yoder. The children had eagerly accepted life on the farm. William rose early each day to help Abraham care for the livestock. Kayla gathered eggs and fed the goats and chickens. The children were flourishing. Color filled their cheeks and their eyes twinkled.

Julia's eyes twinkled, too, and each moment that they were together brought Abraham joy. He could not think about what would happen when she and the children were moved to another location. He had not called Jonathan again, although he and William checked for messages at the phone shack when they cared for his neighbor's animals.

Julia rang the bell, calling them to their noonday meal. He and the children finished the chores they were doing and washed their hands at the pump.

"*Mamm* says we can wash up inside," Kayla announced as she lathered soap in her small hands. "But I like using the pump. It reminds me of the olden days."

Abraham had to smile. "By olden days, do you mean a few years ago?"

She giggled. The sound of her laughter filled him with delight.

"No, I mean the really olden days, like the books I read written by Laura Ingalls Wilder. Do you know her, Mr. Abraham?"

"I do not know her, Kayla. I am not *that* old."

She giggled again. "In her stories, the people wash their hands in well water, too."

"Soon we will go to the library and get more books for you to read."

"William wants books on farming. He says he's going to buy land and grow corn and wheat."

The boy nodded. "And raise horses."

"You are good with the animals, William. In fact, you will make a fine farmer or anything else you chose to do with your life."

"I want to be a teacher when I grow up," Kayla announced. "Sarah's daughter said she will teach at the Amish school. Do you think I can go there next year?"

Abraham handed Kayla the towel. "Your mother will decide about next year. Right now you should study hard and learn as much as you can. Teachers must be very smart so they can teach their students. Therefore you must work hard to learn everything you can."

"Farmers have to be smart, too," William added as he reached for the towel. "Plus they get hungry. Let's go eat."

"I'll race you," Kayla said.

She took off running, but William hung back a few seconds. Abraham appreciated the boy's efforts to let his younger sister win.

Arriving at the porch first, Kayla cheered for herself before she opened the door and stepped into the kitchen.

Abraham approached William and patted his shoulder. "You are becoming a man, William. You put your sister before yourself, which is the mark of a considerate person."

The boy beamed with the praise. "*Mamm* said she is proud of me."

"As she should be." Abraham placed his hand on the boy's shoulder. "I am proud of you, too."

William stood a little straighter. He removed his hat before Abraham pushed open the door.

"It smells like your mother has something good prepared for us to eat."

"I feel like I could eat a bear." William laughed.

"Look at you, William." Julia fussed as she glanced at the door. "You are getting so tall. Each day you grow more."

"Abraham said I am growing faster than the calves."

"The baby chicks grow fast, too," Kayla added. She poured milk for herself and William and waited at the table for her brother to pull out the bench for her.

"Kayla, someday you will have to seat yourself again."

"*Mamm* says it is nice to have a man hold her chair."

Abraham glanced at Julia, who quickly turned toward the stove, but not before he saw her blush. "Your *mamm* is right, Kayla. It is nice when a woman is given the attention she deserves. Your mother works very hard for all of us. If we can find little ways to make her life brighter, we should do that."

"You are much too kind, Abraham."

"Just truthful, Julia." He held her chair as she took her seat.

Julia had fixed sloppy joe sandwiches. The meat and tomato mixture filled the kitchen with a spicy aroma that made his mouth water. Chips, pickles and potato salad waited on the table.

"We will give thanks." Abraham bowed his head.

They lowered their heads and prayed silently. Once he glanced up, Kayla caught his eye and then lowered her head again.

"Did you add an extra prayer?" he asked.

"I asked God for us to stay here with you, Mr. Abraham, forever."

He caught himself as he reached for his glass of water. "Forever is a long time."

"*Yah*." The child gave the reply as if she had been raised Amish her whole life.

"Did God answer your prayer?" Julia asked.

"He said He's working on it."

Julia glanced at Abraham, but she was not smiling. He worried she was wondering how much longer she would have to hole up in Yoder. He had been wrong in not calling Jonathan. Another trip to town might be necessary.

"The Yoder flea market is tomorrow," he announced. "The whole town will be there, along with the people who live in the surrounding area."

Julia passed him the potato salad. "You mentioned agreeing to help Sarah before we showed up on your doorstep."

"I had told her I would help." He dropped a heaping spoonful of the potato salad onto his plate. "You wanted to do something nice for her, Julia. We could help transport her items, and I could also take a few of my neighbor's things to sell."

"I've never been to a flea market." Julia took a bite from her sandwich.

"It would be fun to see the other families," Kayla added.

"William and I will ride to Sarah's house to let her know. You will drive the buggy, William."

The boy's eyes widened. He said nothing but his smile was answer enough. "Should we hurry through lunch?"

Abraham held up his hand. "We have plenty of time. Enjoy the food your mother has prepared."

"There will be a lot of people at the market?" Julia asked.

"Many. I will man a booth. All of you can help me. And we will help Sarah."

"What about our chores?" William asked.

"I like the way you are putting the farm first, William."

The boy smiled at the comment.

"We will rise early and get our work done before we leave."

"Kayla and I can make a picnic lunch," Julia suggested.

"That would be nice, but sometimes it is enjoyable not to cook. There will be food to buy, corn dogs and hamburgers, pizza and apple fritters and funnel cakes."

"I like pizza." Kayla's eyes were wide.

"I do, too," Abraham said. "It is agreed. We will eat lunch there."

Everyone was excited, and Julia seemed to be even more excited than the children.

"You have been holed up here on the farm without having an opportunity to talk to other women," he told her. "I should have thought more about your needs."

"You have thought of nothing other than our needs since we have come here, Abraham. Although I must admit a day in town will be fun. The children are looking forward to it, and so am I."

"Before it gets too late, I must have William drive the buggy to Sarah's house as I promised him."

"He will enjoy the opportunity to guide Buttercup, but are you sure he is ready?"

"Most boys around here are driving teams by age seven or eight. The girls learn early, too."

Julia held up her hand. "Let's wait on Kayla."

"As you wish." He reached for his hat on the peg by the door. "We will not be gone long."

"Tell Sarah I am looking forward to seeing her."

"This I will do."

After giving William thorough instructions on how to handle Buttercup and what to be aware of, he climbed into the buggy seat next to the boy and sat back to enjoy the ride. Julia and Kayla stepped onto the porch and waved farewell.

"We will be back soon," Abraham assured them as the buggy headed away from the farm and onto the main road.

Julia hurried Kayla inside after the buggy drove out of sight. Abraham and William were not going far, but after a couple of hours, Julia became concerned. Probably because her son was holding the reins, and she remembered all too well what had happened outside the grocery.

She checked that the doors to the house were locked and then sat with Kayla at the table to do her lessons. As the child read the directions and marked her workbook, Julia kept glancing at the clock on the wall.

The distance to Sarah's house could not be far, yet at the end of the next hour, when she went to the window to watch for the buggy's return, she saw nothing and no one on the road.

Her stomach flip-flopped as troubling thoughts floated through her mind.

"May I color?" Kayla asked.

"First, read aloud to me."

Kayla pulled a favorite book from the box of school supplies, a story in the *Little House on the Prairie* series, and turned to where she had placed her bookmark.

As her daughter read, Julia fidgeted due to the pent-up energy with which she had trouble dealing.

"Would you like a glass of lemonade?" she asked when Kayla came to the end of the chapter.

"Could we make cookies?"

"Why not?" Anything to keep her mind off the time, and her son and Abraham's failure to return.

Julia turned the baking into a teachable moment. Kayla had to measure the ingredients and then they talked about fractions and how the various parts made up the whole.

Kayla grasped the concepts quickly, although her arm tired when she mixed the dough.

"Will you help me, *Mamm*?"

"Of course. You've done such a good job with measuring everything into the bowl."

"The dough is too stiff," Kayla said as she handed the spoon to Julia.

Mixing the cookies helped Julia get out some of her own frustration.

"Pull the cookie sheet from the cabinet, Kayla."

Using spoons, they dropped round balls of dough onto two baking sheets and placed them in the oven.

"Quickly, now, we must clean up our work area."

Julia wanted everything to look nice when Abraham got home, but as twilight began to fall, she was overcome with worry. She stood at the window peering down the lane and forgot about the cookies until a burning smell alerted her to a problem.

Pulling the pans from the oven and seeing the crisp edges on many of the cookies made her spirits sink even lower. She put the cookies on a rack to cool, thankful some of them were salvageable.

"May I eat one now?" Kayla asked.

"Of course. Sit at the table. I'll pour milk."

As Kayla enjoyed her snack, Julia returned to the window and stared at the road, longing for sight of the buggy.

"Mrs. Fielding told me a watched pot never boils." Kayla brought her plate and glass to the sink and put her hand in her mother's. "I had to ask Mrs. Fielding to explain what that meant. Do you know what it means, Mama?"

Julia looked down at Kayla. "You tell me, honey."

"It means you need to stop worrying about William and Mr. Abraham. They will get home soon, but it won't seem like it's soon if you keep staring out the window."

Julia let out a deep sigh. Kayla was right. Staying busy would help to pass the time and calm her frayed nerves. "Let's get dinner ready," she suggested.

But when the table was set and the pork chops were fried and the leftover potato salad from lunch were all on the table, Julia feared even more for her son and Abraham.

Without a phone, she had no way of contacting them. Even if she used the neighbor's phone, who would she call? Sarah didn't have a phone.

If only she knew how to catch a horse in the pasture and harness it to the other buggy. As much as she enjoyed Amish life, she didn't know the first thing about horses or buggies or how to get herself to Sarah's farm without walking.

She turned to look at Kayla, who was coloring a bright picture of spring flowers. The child could not walk that far, which meant Julia was stuck in the house and would remain here until Abraham and William returned or until someone came to tell her what had happened.

Because she was sure something had happened to them.

Tears burned her eyes. She blinked to keep them back, her heart pounding and her pulse beating much too fast. The top of her head felt like it would explode with the tension that had built up over the last few hours.

Tears wouldn't help, but still they slipped from her eyes. She stepped into the main room so Kayla wouldn't see her. Pulling a tissue from a box, she wiped her eyes and braced her spine, determined to be strong.

But when the door opened and Abraham walked into the kitchen with a smile on his face and a twinkle in his eyes, followed by William who seemed equally jovial, she could no longer hold back her emotions.

"Is everything okay?" she demanded before they had time to hang their hats on the wall pegs.

"*Yah*, why do you ask?"

She pointed to the window. "Because it is almost dark. William was driving the buggy. Anything could have happened."

"William is a *gut* driver. He did a fine job. You would be proud of his ability."

"I am proud of him, but I am not happy about being left in this house and not knowing what was happening."

"Sarah had work that needed to be done," he explained. "She does not have a husband. Some of the neighbors lend a hand, but everyone is busy with their own farms. We loaded the boxes of the items she will sell into her buggy so she will be ready tomorrow. Then she insisted we have a piece of pie."

"Did you not realize I would be worried?"

Abraham stared back at her, clueless. He hadn't realized anything. He probably hadn't thought of her. She was acting like a temperamental child—she knew it—but she couldn't change the way she felt. All the anxiety that had built up, the worry that had turned to fear and eaten at her over the long afternoon came pouring out in a flood of tears.

Confusion covered Abraham's face. William looked worried. Kayla put away her coloring and stood by her mother.

"Mama thought something bad had happened. She has been scared. You should not have been gone so long."

When Abraham failed to say anything, Julia refused to

stand in front of him overcome with embarrassment and a mix of frustration and even anger at herself for thinking the worst when they hadn't thought to come home as quickly as possible. She was glad they could help Sarah. She was a beautiful woman, plus she was Amish and she baked delicious pies. Julia couldn't compete—not that they were in competition.

Abraham and Sarah would be good together. Both Amish. Both had lost their spouses. She could see a look of attraction on Abraham's face when he talked about today's visit and that made Julia even more upset with herself and with him.

"Dinner's on the table," she said, rushing past them and hurrying upstairs. She ran to her bedroom and slammed the door behind her. Then she dropped onto her bed and let the tears fall, knowing she was being foolish and childish and irrational, but she couldn't stop the tears and she couldn't stop the concern that something, someday, would happen to one of them. She had lived with fear for so long that she never seemed able to escape its insidious hold.

In the *Englisch* world, medical personnel would claim she needed counseling. In reality, she just needed to feel safe and secure, and not have to look over her shoulder or worry if her son was late coming home.

She thought things had gotten better, but they hadn't changed. She was still fearful. Danger, even if it wasn't gang related, was rampant in the world. It would never end, and she would never feel safe again.

NINETEEN

Abraham had not wanted the pie, but Sarah had cut slices and set them on the table when he and William finished loading her carriage. She had seemed so eager to offer her thanks that Abraham had agreed to eat quickly. He had seen the twilight and even wondered if Julia would be worried. Why had he not said no to Sarah and come home after the work was done?

The children were silent as they ate dinner, both concerned about their mother.

"She is tired today," Abraham offered as an excuse. "And we stayed away too long. This is a good lesson for all of us to be considerate of your *mamm*."

"I told her about pots boiling," Kayla added, looking older than her years. Although Abraham did not understand her comment, he trusted it had something to do with Julia's upset.

"You children should get to bed early this evening. I will do the dishes. Tomorrow we will rise before dawn. Your mother will feel better, and we will have a wonderful day in town."

"I hope I can sleep, Mr. Abraham, because I'm so excited," Kayla admitted.

He hugged her. "Say your prayers and you will soon be asleep. I will see you in the morning."

She wrapped her arms around his neck and hugged him tight. The warmth of her sweet arms and the smell of her brought back memories of Becca, but instead of overwhelming pain and sorrow, he felt the joy of this precious child who was so forthright and giving. Kayla had captured a part of his heart. Not that she had usurped his own daughter's spot, no one could do that, but his heart was big enough to make room for both of them. That was what made love so special. It did not exclude. The space love held in a person's heart only grew larger, which allowed the capacity to love to grow greater.

Once she had hurried upstairs, Abraham turned to William. "You have worked hard today, you must be tired."

"I am ready to sleep. Thank you, Abraham, for letting me drive the buggy. That is something I never would have learned if we had stayed in Philadelphia."

"You have learned much here."

"Because you have taught me. Don't get upset with Mom. She was worried. I could tell from the look on her face. She would look at me like that when we lived in the city, if I was on the street when she wanted me home. It was the fear of losing me. After what happened in Kansas City, I understand that now."

"Your mother was worried about you today. We should not have stayed so long."

"But Miss Sarah needed help."

"I know. Next time we must think of your mother first."

"Mom likes you, Abraham."

"What?"

"I can tell. Maybe you don't see it because you didn't know her before, but you make her smile, and she's happy here. Even though she was upset today, she is usually less worried here than in the city. I even hear her singing sometimes, which she rarely did before."

"Singing is good." Abraham did not know what else to say. He felt like he was conversing with a peer instead of a boy who could see a change in his mother.

Abraham wished what the boy said was true, but he could not fool himself. Julia was concerned about her son's well-being. Abraham was secondary.

"Tomorrow you need to tell her you're sorry," William said, rising from his chair.

The boy was right. Abraham had not apologized. Shame on him.

William held out his hand. Abraham grasped it, then pulled the boy closer and patted his shoulder. "Sleep well. I will see you in the morning."

"We will not mention that we talked about Mom," William added. "It will be our secret."

William was as wise as his sister, even if he was more reticent. Both children, if they continued on the same path, would do well in life—Abraham felt sure. If only Abraham could remain in their lives long enough to see them mature.

With a heavy sigh, he cleared the table and washed the dishes. He pulled a kitchen towel from a drawer, wiped the plates and utensils dry, and returned them to the cupboard. After folding the towel, he hung it on the rack by the sink and was ready to leave when he heard footsteps on the stairs.

Julia appeared, her hair loose and flowing around her shoulders. Her face was splotched from her tears and her nose was red, but she looked beautiful.

Drawing in a deep breath, he crossed the kitchen to stand in front of her.

"I am sorry," he said. "I was not thinking of you and only thought of getting the work done. As you mentioned, we were both grateful for Sarah taking Kayla in, and I wanted to help today so she would be ready for her sale tomorrow."

"I'm glad you helped her."

"But I never should have had the pie. That was a mistake and one that took more time and made you even more concerned. I will not make that mistake again if you can forgive me."

"Oh, Abraham, I acted like a foolish teenager. Although, thinking of the fine man William seems to have become, that's probably doing an injustice to teens. I let my fears get the best of me. You must forgive me for that. My head knew you were probably safe, but my heart kept asking—if something happened, how would I endure? I was thinking of myself and not you, so I am the one begging to be forgiven."

He opened his arms and she stepped into his embrace. The world stood still, and all he could see was her beautiful face and her upturned lips. Everything within him wanted to pull her even closer and kiss her—not once, but over and over again. He wanted it more than anything, and as he looked more closely, he realized that was what she wanted, as well, which made his knees weak and his heart pound all the more quickly.

"Julia, would you mind if—"

"Kiss me, Abraham. It's what we've both wanted for too long."

As he lowered his lips to hers, he felt a sense of homecoming, as if everything that had caused him pain in the past was over and only the future, a future of hope and happiness, lay ahead.

"Mama?" came Kayla's voice. "I can't sleep."

Julia pulled back, surprise written on her face.

Abraham's euphoria plummeted as she stepped from

his arms. The warmth he had felt dissipated until he was chilled and confused and not sure why he had kissed her.

What was happening to his peaceful life? He had come back to the Amish way to hide out from life, but Julia had opened the door he shut when Marianne and Becca died. Julia had brought light and sunshine and love and laughter back into his broken heart, but he did not deserve any of what she had given him. He had not been able to protect his wife and daughter. He could not be trusted to protect Julia and her children, even if the Philadores had given up their search.

He needed to talk to Jonathan. Perhaps he would call him tomorrow. Julia and her children needed to leavc. As soon as possible.

As she hurried to comfort Kayla, Abraham let himself out through the kitchen door into the cool, crisp night. He walked to the lonely house where he would stay for the rest of his years. The only things he would hold onto were the memories of Julia and her children, and the memory of her in his arms tonight.

Julia woke with the feeling of Abraham's kiss still on her lips. Tired though she was, she had slept little and had tossed and turned for most of the night, wondering what she needed to do. As much as she wanted to stay with Abraham, she knew he didn't need to be saddled with a woman and two children, especially a woman who, although she enjoyed the Amish faith, had a long way to go before she could be accepted through baptism. He didn't need to wait for a wife to care for him when Sarah was so close and so interested in Abraham.

Julia dressed quickly and arranged her hair, grateful that pinning the dress and pulling her hair into a bun had become almost second nature in such a short time.

She hurried downstairs, threw a log on the fire in the woodstove and started the coffee.

William raced down the stairs and into the kitchen as if he were late for a job interview. "Is Abraham already in the barn?"

"I don't know. If so, ask him when he wants breakfast."

The boy grabbed his hat from the wall peg and ran outside without shutting the door. She hurried to close it and spied Abraham hauling feed to the barn. His gaze was warm, causing a tingle to scurry down her spine. For all her concern throughout the night, she couldn't help but smile.

"How long before you'll be ready for breakfast?" she called.

"About forty-five minutes, if that gives you enough time."

"It's perfect. I'm looking forward to the day."

The sun peered over the horizon, its rays as bright as Abraham's smile. "It will be good to be together."

She waved and then closed the door. Being with Abraham would be good, she knew that. Another day together, then she could decide whether to call Jonathan or not. Right now, she wanted to enjoy the moment and enjoy Abraham, no matter how long they had. She would savor this day so she could remember it forever.

Kayla hurried downstairs, wearing her Amish dress. "Can you pull my hair into a bun, *Mamm*?"

"After breakfast, honey. Take the basket and collect the eggs, then see if Abraham needs help with any of the other chores."

The child nearly tripped over her feet in her excitement as she left the house and ran toward the chicken coop. Julia smiled, thinking of the fun her children would have in town. All too soon, she heard a wail from outside and opened the door to see William carrying Kayla in his arms.

Julia's heart lurched with concern. She scurried across the porch and down the steps to join them near the water pump. "Did you fall? Are you hurt?"

"My dress." Fat tears streamed down Kayla's cheeks. She pointed to the raw egg whites mixed with thick yellow yolks and broken shells that covered her clothing. William's shirt was equally soiled from carrying his sister.

"Kayla tried to get eggs from a nest on one of the high rafters," he explained. "The ladder she was standing on gave way. She fell and the eggs in her basket broke."

"Did you hurt yourself?" Julia reached for her daughter and drew Kayla into her arms.

"I'm not hurt," the child said between tears. "But I can't go to town with a dirty dress."

"We can wash your dress," Julia soothed.

Kayla sniffed and wiped her eyes. "But not in time for the flea market."

"You can wear one of the outfits you brought from Philadelphia."

"I won't look Amish and people will wonder why an *Englisch* girl is with an Amish family."

Julia glanced at William's shirt that was stained with egg, and her own bodice that was soiled after coming in contact with Kayla's egg-soaked dress. "We'll all change into our Philadelphia clothes."

Abraham stepped from the barn, no doubt hearing the upset. "Is everything okay?"

"Nothing that can't be fixed with a quick change of clothes. We'll be wearing *Englisch* outfits today."

"Is it okay, Mr. Abraham, if I'm not wearing my Amish dress?" Kayla asked with another sniff.

"What you wear is not important, Kayla. Just so we can all be together."

Julia was grateful for Abraham's calm reassurance that eased Kayla's upset. The child changed into a light-blue dress she claimed was the same color as her Amish outfit. Her face was still puffy and splotched from crying, but she smiled eagerly when they all returned to the kitchen. Abraham and William ate a hearty breakfast, but Kayla was so excited she barely touched her food.

Julia spread butter over a biscuit, added a dollop of strawberry preserves and handed it to her daughter. "Eat this or you'll be hungry later."

"I'm too excited."

"You're excited now, but you'll be hungry later. Sarah and Ella will be here soon. You want to be finished eating and have the table clean before they arrive."

The reminder that work needed to be done before they left for town was all Kayla needed. She quickly ate the biscuit along with a few spoonfuls of egg. Then, after asking to be excused, she cleared the dishes off the table and washed the plates and silverware.

"Thanks for your help," Julia said. "Now go see if Abraham needs you while I wash the pots and pans. If we work together, we'll be ready when our neighbors arrive."

Looking up from the kitchen window, Julia saw William driving the wagon across the road to Mr. Raber's barn. He and Abraham would load the furniture for sale into the rear of it. They returned just as Sarah pulled her mare to a stop by the back porch.

Julia opened the door and called a greeting. "I'll be ready in a minute or two."

She hurried to straighten her hair and slipped a lightweight sweater over her shoulders. When she returned outside, Kayla was talking to Sarah's daughter while the girl's mother laughed at something Abraham had said.

The look that passed between them made Julia realize how perfect Sarah would be for Abraham. Yet his kiss was still fresh on Julia's lips. He probably didn't know what he wanted, an Amish wife or an *Englisch* woman who liked everything about the Amish way of life.

Such thoughts needed to be saved for another day. At the moment, they needed to get to town to claim the two tables that would showcase their wares and draw customers.

Julia hugged Sarah and Ella. "William and Kayla, wash your hands and faces, and then we'll be on our way."

They hurried inside and returned so quickly that Julia wondered if they had complied with her instructions. Wisely, she decided not to ask if they had used soap.

Abraham helped her climb onto the front seat of his wagon and assisted Sarah and Ella into their buggy. Kayla and William sat behind Julia. With a flip of the reins, Abraham steered Buttercup toward town.

Kayla asked William questions about what they might see. As the children talked, Julia leaned closer to Abraham. "I'm sorry about my upset yesterday," she said, keeping her voice low.

"That was my fault totally, and again, I apologize, but today is a new day, *yah*?"

"It is that and a beautiful day for a drive."

"You said yesterday that you have never been to a flea market."

"Is it like a garage sale?" she teased.

He laughed. "This is far larger with many more things for sale. Produce from the gardens, although only spring vegetables are available now. You will find all types of wares both new and used. Farm equipment and handmade items."

"Like your neighbor's furniture."

"And the many items Sarah has stitched."

"She is an accomplished seamstress."

Abraham's brow furrowed and his lips turned into an impish grin. "Sarah is a neighbor, Julia. Nothing more."

The look he flashed her took Julia's breath. She glanced at the road and scooted over a bit to distance herself from his magnetism. Why was she so taken at times with him? Yet, at other times, like yesterday, he unsettled her peace and calm.

"How long until we get there, Mr. Abraham?" Kayla questioned from the rear.

"It will not be long. Why not sing us a song as we ride?"

Kayla began singing a child's tune about going to town and buying a toy so she could give it to a girl or boy who didn't have toys. The song's lyrics were simple, but the message was important for children to embrace as their own.

When she stopped singing, she laughed.

"What's so funny?" Julia asked, turning toward her daughter.

"We have everything we wanted, Mama. William is not in a gang, we have space to run and skip and jump, we have a nice house and food to eat, and a pretty dress for me to wear."

Her daughter's gratitude was contagious. "You're so right, Kayla. We have everything we need."

TWENTY

Abraham was glad they had started for town early. By thc time they approached the first intersection, the line of traffic was backed up for an entire block. Slowly they moved forward, part of a long trail of wagons and buggies interspersed with a few cars and pickups that waited to turn into the flea market.

A huge steel barn-type structure stretched across the center of the expansive property. To the side, horses were tethered to hitching poles and more horses grazed in a rear pasture.

As soon as they were able to turn in, Sarah pulled her buggy to a stop behind them. They found the man overseeing the flea market who showed them to their assigned tables. Abraham's area opened toward the stables where he had rented a stall for Buttercup.

He and William hauled the larger pieces from the wagon while Julia and Kayla moved Sarah's quilts and other handmade items into her area. After unhitching Buttercup, Abraham and William settled the mare in the barn and then returned to the table to set up the wares. Julia had already arranged the majority of the merchandise.

"It looks so inviting," she told them as she looked over the two tables.

"Only because of your eye for decorating, Julia. I have a suspicion we will sell a lot of Mr. Raber's items."

"Are you a woodworker, Abraham?"

He shrugged, unwilling to delve into his own talents. "I used to do woodworking and thought I might embrace it as a productive hobby, but after my wife and daughter passed, I gave that up."

"You should start again," she encouraged him. "Especially if it was something you enjoyed doing."

He did like working with his hands, but he had given it up more as a personal sacrifice after what had happened. If Marianne and Becca had lost their lives because of him, he no longer deserved to do anything that lifted his spirits or brought joy to his life. It was ironic that Julia had mentioned something that once brought him pleasure.

"How about a cup of coffee?" Abraham asked, needing to turn the conversation away from his past.

"That sounds perfect."

He hurried to the stall across from them and returned with coffee for Julia and Sarah along with a cup for himself. "Children, would you like hot chocolate?"

"*Yah*," the two girls squealed.

William nodded. "Yes, please."

Abraham laughed. "I should have known." Taking the children with him, he purchased a hot drink for each of them and carried Kayla's back to their table to ensure it did not spill. The children sat on folding chairs and enjoyed their hot chocolate as people started to enter the large, open area.

Sarah's quilts were a hit, and she soon had a gathering of women examining her stitches and admiring the patterns. Julia helped her and then returned to aid Abraham when Mr. Raber's furniture attracted customers.

The children stayed close and helped as best they could.

Kayla met some other children who were with their parents at nearby booths, and all of them sat in a circle and ate pizza for lunch washed down with lemonade.

"Could we have a funnel cake?" Kayla pleaded with her mother after she had finished her pizza. The sugary sweet smell of funnel cakes filled the arena, and even Abraham's mouth watered.

"You had a very large slice of pizza," Julia reminded the child.

"But the funnel cake is for dessert."

"Perhaps in a bit."

At the next lull in the crowd of buyers, Abraham grabbed Kayla's hand and walked her to the booth at the opposite end of the market.

"Your mother said you could have dessert in a bit. I do believe a bit of time has passed. Would a funnel cake be good?"

"Oh, yes, Mr. Abraham. Funnel cake would be wonderful."

"You will share with William and Ella?"

"I will share with everyone."

Abraham could not refuse the adorable child who had worked her way so quickly into his heart. William had a spot there, as well. The boy was becoming someone Abraham could count on to help him with the farm. For the last three years, Abraham had worked alone. Having William with him in the barn, mending fences, checking the cattle, made the days pass more quickly and the work more enjoyable.

Soon the fields would need to be plowed. He was eager to teach William how to guide the draft horses to make straight rows for the new crops.

"You should sit and relax for a while," he told Julia. She was pouring her heart and soul into the flea market, and her ability amazed him. She even took orders for his neighbor, convincing customers who were merely looking that a kitchen table or chairs or a cabinet would be perfect for their homes. Sales continued throughout the afternoon, and they made more money than at previous flea markets.

"You are a natural," Abraham told her.

"I just know a good thing when I see it, and your neighbor's furniture is lovely and is being sold at a reasonable price. Anyone would be foolish to let such an opportunity pass by, which is what I tell people who stop by the table."

"Mr. Raber will be pleasantly surprised that so many pieces sold."

"He has good merchandise, Abraham. Next year you need to have your own items for sale."

Sarah went to get a sandwich and left her daughter and Kayla to watch the table. A man approached with a camera around his neck. Abraham recognized him as the guy who had stopped by the phone shack to ask directions.

"How much is this quilt?" the man asked Ella.

"Three hundred dollars."

"That's too expensive. What about this other one?"

The girl checked the price tag affixed to the label. "That one is for a king-sized bed. It sells for three hundred and fifty dollars."

"Are there any cheap quilts?"

Julia moved closer to help. "You mean smaller quilts that sell for less?" She pointed to a lovely pattern made in blue calico.

"That's what I mean. Listen, I don't want to cause trouble, but I need some photos. You don't mind if I take pictures of the quilts with that young Amish girl who's manning the table?"

Before she could say anything, he lifted the camera

from around his neck and started to snap some shots of Sarah's daughter.

Julia took Kayla's hand and backed her away from the table.

Spying Kayla, the guy smiled and raised his camera. "What an adorable little girl."

"No." Abraham placed his hand over the lens, startling the man.

"What are you doing?" The guy squared his shoulders.

"No pictures. Amish do not allow photographs."

The man looked angry initially and then calmed. "I've heard that before, but the little girl's not Amish."

"She is a friend of the Amish and the same rule applies to her." Abraham leaned closer to the man. "If you have heard of our ways, why did you attempt to take pictures?"

The guy stared at Abraham, slack-jawed. "I…I'm not sure."

"You are not sure because your need for photographs is more important than our desire not to have pictures taken?"

"I didn't mean to cause a problem."

"You need to respect our ways just as we respect yours."

"Look, I'm sorry. A guy told me to get lots of pictures."

"Who is that guy?"

The man shrugged. "He's someone staying at the same hotel. He said I could sell the photos online."

"Did you take any knowingly of the Amish?"

"Just the girl with the quilts, but I'll delete those." The guy held up his camera. "You can check my photo file."

Seeing remorse in the man's eyes, Abraham glanced quickly through the more recent photos, deleted a few that included Sarah's daughter and then handed the camera back to the owner.

The man turned to Julia. “In hopes of making amends, I would like to buy one of the smaller quilts. The green one will look nice in my living room.”

“You are from around here?” she asked.

“I flew in on business last week and rented a car so I could see some of this area of the country.”

“You are the part-time travel writer,” Abraham said, knowing the man had failed to make the connection.

The guy smiled. “I knew you looked familiar. Look, I’m sorry about the photographs, but pictures sell. You know what I mean?”

“Where’s home?” Julia asked.

“Philadelphia.”

The mention of Philadelphia unsettled Abraham. Even if Pablo and Mateo were dead, William could still be in danger. He should have studied the man’s digital photo file more closely.

“Have a safe trip home,” Julia said, her face pale and her gaze wary.

The man hurried to another stall. Abraham saw him snap a few photographs, but of the entire area instead of singling out specific people.

By late afternoon, the crowds had started to diminish and Julia and Abraham sat behind their table, sipping coffee.

Sarah was talking to ladies she knew and Ella was visiting with girls her own age.

“You should take Kayla for a walk around the area,” Abraham suggested. “I will do the same with William after you return. Outside in the rear, they usually have puppies for sale.”

“That’s not what we need,” she laughed. “Especially when we don’t know how long we’re staying.”

Her face grew serious and Abraham turned away, wishing he had not mentioned the pups.

"Perhaps someday, when you are settled," he added, hoping to smooth over the rough edges of her comment.

"You won't mind us leaving you?"

Abraham hesitated, not sure of what she meant.

"Leaving you here at the table with William?" she hastily added.

"Not at all. In fact, he might want to go with you."

But when she asked, the boy opted to remain with Abraham.

Kayla took her mother's hand and the two slowly made their way from booth to booth, examining everything for sale.

"Have you enjoyed the day, William?" Abraham asked.

"Yah, it is different but *gut*. I heard some of the boys around my age talking about plowing the fields and planting."

"It is almost that time."

"I wondered if you would teach me."

Abraham nodded. "We will do that together if you are still here when it is time to plant."

"I hope we're still here."

Abraham hoped so, too. He watched Julia make her way through the crowd of people. She stood out, but not because of her *Englisch* clothing. Perhaps it was the way she held herself or her laughter or the way she had found a spot in his life. He wanted her to stay in his life, along with her children.

Abraham handed William a few dollars. "The man in the booth across the way has some carrots for sale. Buy half a bushel and then take a couple to Buttercup. I know she would like to see you."

William face lit up. "*Danke*." He hurried over with the money and bought the carrots.

The barn sat adjacent to the market and the crowd was thinning. William grabbed two of the carrots and left the half bushel beside Abraham before walking toward the barn. Abraham nodded approvingly. Buttercup and the boy would enjoy being together.

Abraham needed to keep focused on today and not think about what might happen in the days ahead. Live life in the present, which was what he was trying to do.

Kayla was enamored with the puppies and begged to have one.

"Someday, perhaps, but right now we are still unsettled," Julia tried to explain.

"Look how little they are."

"You can hold them." The Amish lady selling the puppies placed two in Kayla's arms.

She cuddled the puppies and giggled as they squirmed and licked her neck. "They're so cute."

"And not housebroken," Julia pointed out.

"I could ask Abraham. He bought me funnel cake today."

Julia narrowed her gaze. "*Kayla May,* the funnel cake was a treat. A puppy would be with us for a long time. You will not ask Abraham. He has a big heart, but we do not want to infringe on his good nature."

"He likes animals."

"You're right. I'm sure he likes dogs, but these puppies will find a home with someone else."

Reluctantly, her daughter handed them back to the lady and then took Julia's hand.

"There's William." Kayla pointed to the barn as William entered. "He just went inside. He was holding carrots. He probably went to see Buttercup. May we go too, *Mamm*?"

Visiting Buttercup was a good trade-off, especially if it took Kayla's mind off the puppies. Julia had to admit they were sweet, but she had two children to care for. She wasn't ready to take on a pet.

A number of buggies had already left the flea market. Soon Abraham would want to load the wagon and head home. As much as she and the children had enjoyed the day, Julia knew it was time to leave.

"We'll see Buttercup and then return to help Abraham. He will need to pack up soon," she said to prepare Kayla, knowing it would be hard to have today come to a close.

The barn was dark when they stepped inside. Julia heard a shuffle that worried her. "William?"

He didn't answer. She hesitated, trying to adjust to the darkness.

Someone groaned. Her heart raced. "William, where are you?"

Something heavy slammed against one of the stalls. She ran, fearing for her son.

"Kayla," Julia called over her shoulder. "Get Abraham. Hurry."

The child hesitated, her eyes wide.

"Go! Now!"

Julia raced from one stall to another, looking for William.

A back door opened. Light broke through the darkness.

She stopped, unsure of what she saw. Realization hit hard. A man had his hands around her son's neck and was pulling him through the open doorway.

She raced forward and grabbed his arm.

He turned.

Pablo?

"Let go of my son."

He pushed her away.

She lunged and dug her fingernails into his cheeks.

"Agh!" Pablo's hold on William loosened.

Her son collapsed onto the straw-covered floor, coughing.

A car waited outside, the motor running. Mateo peered at them from the driver's seat.

"What are you doing?" she screamed at Pablo. "You've got a mother who loves you. You're breaking her heart."

"I need to prove that I'm a man." He grabbed Julia and started to drag her out of the barn toward the car. She kicked and bit his hand.

Mateo opened the driver's door. "Where's the kid?"

"Run, William!" she screamed. "Get away."

Dazed, the boy regained his footing and staggered toward her. "Mom?"

Pablo tightened his hold on Julia.

Removing a ballpoint pen from her pocket, she shoved it into his neck. He sputtered, released his hold on her and took a step back.

Mateo reached for William. The boy stumbled away from him.

Footsteps sounded, running toward them. Julia looked up to see Abraham.

TWENTY-ONE

Pablo and Mateo raced to their car. They climbed in, slammed the doors and squealed away from the barn.

Abraham reached for her. “Are you hurt?”

Julia shook her head and tried to catch her breath. “Only frightened. It was Pablo and Mateo. I… I thought both of them were dead.”

She dropped to the ground where William had fallen.

“I’m okay,” he told them as they helped him up.

“What happened?” Abraham asked.

“I gave Buttercup the carrots and then heard a noise behind me. Before I could see who it was, Pablo jumped me. He said I needed to go back to Philly with him.”

Julia looked at Abraham. “Jonathan’s information about Pablo and Mateo was wrong.”

“Maybe Pablo started the rumor so we would let down our guard.”

One of the deputy sheriffs hurried into the barn. “Someone said there had been trouble.”

“A guy was throwing his weight around.” Abraham put his hand on William’s shoulder. “This young man was in the way.”

He provided a description of Pablo and Mateo and the car they were driving. “Both guys are members of a Philadelphia street gang. If you see them around town, haul them in for questioning. They need to be in jail and off the streets."

A crowd had started to form in the stable, which was something Abraham did not want. He gave the sheriff his address and then squeezed Julia's hand.

"I will hitch up the wagon," he told her. "We need to go home."

She wrapped her arm around William's shoulders and walked back to the market.

Abraham had not been able to protect them. If Kayla had not run to warn him, William and Julia could have been long gone before Abraham had realized they were missing.

His stomach soured at the thought.

He had to call Jonathan. Julia and her children were no longer safe in Yoder. It was a good thing they had been wearing *Englisch* clothing today, so Pablo and Mateo would not look for them within the Amish community. At least, not tonight. New arrangements needed to be made for their safety—new identities and a new place to live, far from Yoder and far from Abraham. As much as he did not want them to leave, he wanted them to be safe, and they were not safe with him.

Julia felt like an arctic blast of frigid air had frozen her heart. The temperature was dropping, but more than that, she was cold from the near capture of her son. How could she and Abraham have believed the rumors that Jonathan heard in Philadelphia? Rumors were never reliable, yet they had wanted to have all this behind them so they had bought into the lies that were circulated.

The gangs had said a third person died in the street

fight, which had been a lie, too. She had been foolish, again. This time it had almost cost William his life.

Abraham stopped to call Jonathan on the way home. The marshals were working on new identities for them. Hopefully they would leave soon. Maybe Abraham could go with them to another Amish community. Hiding within the plain world would have worked, if William had not called David. At least her son had learned a valuable lesson and would never do anything as foolish or dangerous again.

Sarah and her daughter followed behind them in their buggy. Abraham and Julia made sure they were safely at her house, with the few items Sarah had not sold taken inside, before they said goodbye.

Although they tried to make light of everything, Sarah seemed keenly aware that something was afoot. "Whatever happened, Julia, it has been a joy to get to know you and your wonderful children. We will not say goodbye, for we will meet again."

Sarah knew they would be leaving, even without being told. How many other people would soon know if the sheriff started to put it all together?

Abraham's house and the *dawdy* house were dark against the night when they turned into the drive. A sliver of a moon peered through the clouds and cast the houses in long shadows that made the once-welcoming homes appear sinister and foreboding.

Julia clutched her hands to her heart. She didn't need to give fear free rein, not after the turmoil she had been in yesterday. She had learned her lesson and would take each day as it came.

The children were downcast as they climbed from the wagon. William helped Abraham unload the rest of the neighbor's items and unhitch Buttercup, while Kayla and

Julia hurried to fix something light to eat before the children went to bed. Abraham stayed outside longer than expected, and when he entered the house, he nodded to her as if to offer assurance that no one had trespassed on his property.

He remained alert during dinner and excused himself a number of times to step onto the porch and stare into the night. The children played with their food, each somber and concerned.

"Are we leaving?" Kayla asked.

"We will know more tomorrow," Julia told her. "You do not need to be concerned or frightened tonight."

"But that man tried to hurt you and William."

Julia pulled Kyla close. "He didn't hurt us. We are here with you, sweet girl. Do not think of what could have been, think only of the moment and that we are all together."

"If we move, maybe we can get a puppy."

"Did you see puppies today?" Abraham asked when he came back inside. He seemed glad for something to distract them from what had happened.

"The lady let me hold two of them." Kayla rubbed her cheek. "They licked me and cuddled close. One was a wiggle worm, but the other stayed in my arms. That's the puppy I wanted."

"Perhaps someday," he said, which was what Julia had told Kayla.

William wasn't interested in talking about the puppies. He looked scared and tired.

"You need to go to bed, children. Everything will be better in the morning."

At least, Julia hoped it would.

When she checked on the children a few minutes later, William was asleep, and Kayla was drifting off. She had found Annie, the doll that she had ignored for the last few days and had her clasped in her arms as if offering security. At least her daughter had something to hold on to. Julia wished she had something, too.

She stepped back into the kitchen. Abraham had washed the dishes and was drying them and putting them away in the cupboard.

"I have a feeling most Amish men don't wash the dishes," she said.

He smiled. She saw the fatigue on his face and her heart went out to him.

"It's been a long day," she offered.

"I am sorry, Julia."

"Sorry because two men want to do us harm? I'm sorry, too, Abraham, but they have nothing to do with you. You've been our guardian through it all. You took me to Kansas City and found William. Somehow, rather ingeniously, you worked with Grant to get us safely out of the shelter and to the rendezvous with Randy. From everything Jonathan had told us, why wouldn't we think that the search for us was over?"

"I need to check Raber's phone. Jonathan said he would call me back."

"About what happened?"

"About what he thinks we need to do next."

Julia liked his mention of *we*. Whatever the future held, she wanted it to include Abraham. He was thinking the same way she was, which warmed her heart.

"You'll let me know what Jonathan says?"

"Of course, Julia. It should not take long."

She stood at the door as he left, and then stepped onto the porch and watched as he crossed the road.

The farm was quiet and the moon peered ever so slightly through the clouds as Abraham entered the phone shack. As much as she had enjoyed the farm, Julia was resigned to moving on. As long as Abraham was with her, she could manage anything. Without him, she doubted she could take even one step forward.

She went back inside the house and made a fresh pot of coffee. Sarah had given them a pie in thanks for their help today. The children had been too tired for dessert, but she felt sure Abraham would enjoy a slice while they discussed the news Jonathan would share.

She had been foolish to think Abraham should stay with Sarah, especially when Julia needed him and her children did, as well. God had brought him into their lives for a reason. She realized that now.

The rich aroma of the brewed coffee and the cozy glow of the oil lamp brought a comfortable warmth to the kitchen where she felt so at home. If only the sheriff would apprehend Pablo and Mateo. The marshals could deal with the two gang members while Julia and Abraham went on with their lives.

Then she thought of the Philadores and what would happen if they learned Pablo was still alive. Would they search for William again? And, if so, would they find him?

"This is Jay." The message on the answering machine sounded in the small phone shack. "I'd like to buy a kitchen table in maple with six chairs. Call me to confirm the order."

Abraham deleted the coded message from Jonathan. He called the predetermined number and waited for the marshal to answer.

"I had almost given up on hearing from you tonight," Jonathan said in lieu of a greeting. "We've been in contact with the Yoder sheriff. He hasn't apprehended Pablo, which means he and his friend are on the loose. You need to be careful."

"What did you decide about Julia and the children?"

"We're preparing new identities for them. I'll be there in the morning. Tell them to pack and be ready to leave."

Abraham's gut tightened at the thought of having to say goodbye. As much as he did not want them to go, they needed to start a new life for themselves far from Yoder and the Amish community and far from him. He had been a detriment instead of an asset. Jonathan must have realized that or he would have suggested Abraham travel with the family.

"We will be waiting for you, Jonathan."

He hung up, feeling a huge weight settle on his shoulders. Telling Julia would be hard, but he had been in difficult situations before. Seeing Becca's small casket positioned in the church next to his wife's had been the hardest day of his life. He had survived. He would survive this, too.

He hurried across the road and knocked gently on Julia's door. Her face was filled with anticipation when she opened the door and motioned him inside.

"I made a fresh pot of coffee. I'll pour a cup and slice Sarah's pie. Sit at the table, Abraham. I see the fatigue in your eyes. You can eat while you tell me what Jonathan said."

"A cup of coffee sounds good, Julia, but no pie."

She poured two cups and took them to the table. He sat next to her. "Jonathan talked to the sheriff. He and his deputies are still looking for Pablo and Mateo. So far they have come up empty-handed. Perhaps the two gang members have left town and are headed back to Philadelphia."

"If only, although that seems too good to be true."

Abraham agreed, but he said nothing of the sort. Julia

had been frightened today and rightfully so. He did not want to scare her even more.

"The marshals are putting together another identity for you. Jonathan will be here tomorrow morning."

"Then we only have one night to be concerned about our safety."

"Pablo did not know where to find you earlier. It is doubtful he has learned your whereabouts since then, especially with law enforcement looking for him and his buddy."

"I'll pack our bags. Did Jonathan give you any idea of the time he would arrive?"

"I am not sure he knew."

"What about closing down your houses? Who will take care of your livestock?"

Abraham raised his brow. "What are you saying, Julia?"

"I'm saying I will help you with whatever needs to be done before you leave with us."

He shook his head. "I am not going with you. My farm is here. I must stay."

"But you said *we* earlier. What *we* would do. You were going to ask Jonathan what *we* would do next."

"If I said that, I meant it in a general way. You and your children will settle in an *Englisch* community. An Amish man would not fit in."

"I thought Jonathan said we would be safer with the Amish?"

"But that has not been the case, now, has it? You have not been safe here."

"We were fine until William ran away and then Pablo came looking for him. You weren't the problem, Abraham. My son was."

Abraham did not know how to respond. Julia was not

thinking rationally. She had relied on him to get her to Kansas City, but Abraham had not been able to get them out of danger. If not for Grant and his buddies, there was no telling what would have happened.

Today at the flea market, Abraham had been oblivious to the danger. He used to be a good cop, but his skills were rusty, and he was no longer a protector or guardian. He could work a farm, but little more.

Surely Julia saw him for who he truly was, and if she did not, he would ensure she did not make a mistake by thinking he needed to tag along with her and her children. Much as he wanted to be with them, it was not a wise decision. Julia would come to her senses and be grateful to be free from him and his Amish community as soon as she settled in her new location.

"It is late," he said. "You need to sleep."

He stood and started for the door. She grabbed his arm. He stopped and turned to face her, seeing the upset in her gaze.

"Don't think of me," she said, her voice breaking with emotion. "But what about William and Kayla? How can you walk away from them?"

"Julia, it is not what I want, but you are no longer safe here. The children will adjust."

"Adjust." She tried to laugh, but it came out like a cry. "William's father abandoned him and never took time to find out what a great kid his son was. As much as I try to tell him that his dad was mixed-up and thinking only of himself, it still hurts. William opened his heart to you. Don't you see that? Kayla did, as well, only she was more vocal about her feelings."

"I did not want them to depend on me, Julia. They are great kids who will grow into wonderful adults. You have been the one guiding them. You will continue to provide the love and support they need."

"They need a man in their lives, a father figure to encourage them and teach them. You did that all so well, and in just a few days they've bonded with you."

"They will bond with someone else, perhaps someone you will love and marry."

"What?" Julia did not seem to accept what he was saying. "I made a terrible mistake falling in love the first time, Abraham. I will not make that mistake again."

Her words made him bristle. For half a heartbeat, he had thought she was interested in him, but she was adamant about never loving again. He needed to accept what she said as truth.

With a heavy sigh, he turned to the door, removed his hat from the peg and left the house. She locked the door behind him. The sound cut him to the quick as if she were locking him out of her life.

How had he gotten her signals so mixed up?

The temperature was dropping and the clouds covered the moon. He stared at the sky and lifted up a weak prayer. *Lord, give me the strength to carry on.*

Before heading home, he circled the barn, the outbuildings and the *dawdy* house to make certain no one was there, hiding in the shadows, waiting to do Julia and her children harm.

TWENTY-TWO

Julia couldn't cry. She was too hurt and too angry, and the tears wouldn't come. All this time, she had sensed a connection with Abraham. Hadn't they kissed, and hadn't the feelings between them seemed to heighten as the days passed? But it was all pretending on his part. She felt embarrassed and foolish to have been so wrong about him.

He enjoyed his Amish life and had probably been longing for the day when she and the children would be gone.

She pulled their suitcases from the alcove in the hallway. Tomorrow they would dress again in *Englisch* clothing. She would leave the Amish dresses and William's slacks and shirt behind. If she had time, she would wash them and hang them on the line to dry. Abraham could pass them on to a needy family or give them back to Sarah.

Perhaps Julia's suspicions had been right. Sarah was in love with Abraham. Before long, she would be back in his life. A friend, he had called her, but many romances started in friendship. With time, Abraham would see the fine qualities Sarah possessed. Plus, she was Amish.

Julia had liked everything she had seen about the Amish faith. If only Abraham had asked her if she would consider being baptized, because Julia would have told him yes. The Amish faith would have been good for her children, as well.

What would she tell William and Kayla? The wall of frustration broke apart when she thought of her children being hurt again. Tears filled her eyes and spilled down her cheeks.

Her father had been a rough guy who never showed love or appreciation. Julia had left him to marry Charlie, thinking he would be a caring and supportive partner to walk beside through life. But Charlie had thought more about himself than his children or his wife.

Reflecting on her life, she realized how God had intervened to help her so many times. The Lord had been there all along. She was the one who had closed Him out of her heart.

Forgive me, Lord. She hung her head, overcome by her own self-centeredness.

How had she been so wrong about everything and everyone? All too quickly she had dropped her guard and opened her heart to Abraham. Was she so needy that she fell for any man who crossed her path?

She packed the few things they had into the suitcases, then laid out regular clothing for them to wear the next day. When she looked at their Amish outfits, her heart broke for all they would leave behind, most especially Abraham.

She hauled the suitcases downstairs and heated water for tea. A cup of the soothing herbal mix would calm her frayed spirit so she could sleep, at least for a few hours. Tomorrow would be a difficult day.

Cup in hand, she extinguished the oil lamp and stared through the window. As she watched, the clouds rolled across the sky and the moon peered down, washing the farm in moonlight. Such a beautiful area, with its green fields and tall trees and the small creek that ran along the edge of the farm.

If it hadn't been so late, she would have taken her tea onto the porch, but with Pablo and Mateo on the loose, she needed to be cautious.

Instead, she stood at the kitchen sink and sipped her tea, thinking of everything good that had happened since she and her children had arrived at the farm. The memories brought a smile to her lips, but also a heaviness to her heart, knowing she would have to say goodbye to this idyllic spot tomorrow.

She placed the cup on the counter and was ready to return to her bedroom when a movement caught her eyes. Leaning forward, she narrowed her gaze. What had she seen?

The clouds rolled across the moon, cutting off the shimmering light. Surely her eyes were playing tricks on her.

She was starting to turn away when the clouds moved again. Her gaze zeroed in on the nearby pasture and two figures who stood in the tall grass.

Even from this distance, she recognized Pablo and Mateo.

Abraham stepped onto the porch. He quietly closed the door behind him and stared into the night. His gaze focused on the two young men approaching the house. Slowly he moved toward the water pump near the *dawdy* house and waited until they'd rounded the barn.

"Get off my property," Abraham said, his voice raised.

Both guys stopped and stared into the darkness.

Abraham stepped from the shadows. "Get off my property now."

"Hey, man. We wanna talk to Will." Pablo shrugged as if they were doing nothing wrong. "Tell him Davey misses him."

"I will tell the sheriff you are both trespassing."

"And how will you contact the sheriff?" Mateo chuckled. "You Amish don't have phones." He pulled his cell from his pocket. "You wanna use mine?"

"I *wanna* see you turn around, Mateo, and head back to your car parked by the road."

"Oh, man, you're scaring me." Mateo jiggled his knees. "You have me quaking in my boots."

"Leave. Now."

The punk shook his head. "Not without the kid."

"You need better intel," Abraham taunted. "The Philadores called off the search."

"Man, we don't care about the Philadores. We wanna work for the Delphis. Bringing the kid back to Philly will make us important to our *new* brothers." Mateo jabbed his thumb against his chest. "We'll have status."

"Using a kid for your own gain?" Abraham turned to Pablo. "Did your mother raise you to hide behind children?"

"Leave my mother outta this."

"What about your dad, Pablo? Is he proud of you?"

"My dad left me. He didn't care about me or my brother. That's why I have to be *the man*."

"Then be *the man*," Abraham said. "Walk away before someone gets hurt."

Mateo glanced at Pablo. "You're crazy *loco* to listen to him, bro. I'll show him who's in charge." He pulled a nine millimeter from his waistband.

Julia stepped onto the porch.

Abraham raised his hand. "Get back, Julia. Go in the house. Lock the door."

She ignored the warning and moved closer. "Mateo is using you, Pablo. He wants William so he can turn him in to Fuentes. Mateo didn't leave the Philadores. He was in my apartment the night they came looking for Will. The police had Mateo in custody. Ask him how he got off."

"Shut up," Mateo growled.

"Fuentes used his money and power to spring him." Julia took another step forward. "It's true, isn't it, Mateo?"

The punk snarled. "If we can't get your kid, we'll take you back, lady."

"No." Pablo held up his hand. "She's not who we want."

"She's who I want, bro. But I want her dead." He raised his weapon.

Abraham pushed Julia behind the pump.

Mateo fired.

Abraham groaned and grabbed his side.

The door to the house opened. "Mom?"

"No, Will!" Julia screamed. "Stay inside."

Mateo raised his revolver.

Pablo grabbed his arm. "Don't hurt the kid. He's a friend of Davey's."

"As if I care, Pablo. You need to know who's boss."

As the thugs argued, Abraham put his arm around Julia and hurried her to the porch. He grabbed William's hand and urged both of them into the house.

"We're in this together," Pablo insisted.

"No, bro." Mateo laughed. "I'm in this alone. The Philadores don't think the kid's alive, so when I bring him back, I'll be a hero."

He raised his revolver and pulled the trigger.

Pablo took the hit and gasped. He yanked a weapon from his own waistband and fired.

Mateo's eyes bulged. Blood darkened his shirt. He grabbed his gut and fired again.

Pablo groaned with the second hit. His eyes widened, his body twitched and then fell limp onto the ground.

Mateo turned his weapon on Abraham. He squeezed the trigger. The gun jammed. He threw it aside and ran.

Abraham stumbled down from the porch. He kicked the gun away from Pablo and followed Mateo, his gait unsteady.

"Get the guns, Julia," Abraham called over his shoulder. "Ring the dinner bell, Will."

He grasped his side, feeling the warm blood seep into his hand. He had to get Mateo before he escaped again. The Philadelphia gangs knew nothing about Julia and William hiding with the Amish. Abraham had to ensure they never learned of the family's whereabouts. Julia and William would not be safe until Mateo was stopped.

Mateo tripped. He struggled to get his footing.

The clang of the dinner bell echoed in the night.

Abraham's side burned like fire. His legs grew weak, but he continued on, unwilling to give up.

Mateo's car was parked in a stand of trees near the road. He opened the car door and reached for a back-up revolver on the console.

Abraham grabbed the guy's shoulder.

The punk turned, raised the weapon and fired.

The bullet hit Abraham in the gut. He stumbled back, gasping for air.

Mateo climbed into his car and gunned the engine.

Abraham could not stop him. Once again, he had failed.

The last thing he did was call Julia's name.

Julia ran to Abraham and shoved her hand down on his wound, stemming the flow of blood. He wasn't breathing, wasn't moving. William had found Pablo's cell phone and called 911. But would help arrive in time?

The sound of horses' hooves filled the night. She

looked up to see buggies blocking the road. Mateo laid on the horn and swerved around the blockade. His car skidded into a giant oak. He was thrown from the car and landed face down on the ground. Two Amish men ran toward him. They turned him over and shook their heads.

His car horn continued to blare in the night. Over that sound came the shrill scream of sirens.

Two ambulances and the sheriff's car appeared in the distance. One ambulance stopped to check on Mateo. The other skirted the buggies and headed toward Julia.

The EMTs jumped from their vehicle and hurried to her aid. "We've got this, ma'am."

She fell back and stared at her hands covered with Abraham's blood.

William was suddenly next to her, burying his face in her shoulder, crying his eyes out.

"Oh, Mom, he's dead. Abraham is dead."

TWENTY-THREE

Kayla clutched her doll. She hadn't spoken since Julia had awakened her and gotten her dressed. William was ashen. He refused to eat and had only taken a sip of water, claiming he felt sick. Julia could relate. Her head pounded and her puffy eyes burned from the tears she had shed. She had changed out of her blood-soaked clothing and now wore the jeans and sweater she'd had on the night she arrived at Abraham's house. Everything seemed so déjà vu, except in reverse.

They had left the *dawdy* house in a van. Jonathan told her where they were going, but she hadn't listened and didn't care. Stacy and Karl sat in the rear, whispering quietly between themselves. Julia couldn't make out what they said. She turned to glance at them and saw their hands entwined. On any other night, Julia would have taken delight in their new relationship. Tonight, she could think only of Abraham.

He hadn't died, as William had thought, but he was holding on to life by a thread. Mateo and Pablo had both succumbed to their wounds, and the Philadores seem oblivious to what had happened. Still, Jonathan was convinced they couldn't take chances. Not when William's life was on the line. As much as she hadn't want to leave Yoder, Jonathan had given her no choice.

The marshals had pieced together enough information to realize that Pablo thought Mateo was interested in joining the Delphis when Mateo was only thinking of a way to get noticed by Fuentes.

Pablo and Mateo had met the guy with the camera at the Yoder hotel and questioned him about the interesting sights in the area. He talked about a teenage boy and young girl caught on a runaway buggy. Pablo provided a photo of William taken in Philadelphia. The man recognized the boy and provided directions to the farm.

Julia didn't have the wherewithal to fight anymore, except she had to take care of her children. Still, her heart broke, knowing Abraham might not survive.

Please, Lord, save him. Guide the doctors and nurses who care for him. Heal his wounds and let him live.

"We're here."

She glanced at Jonathan. "I thought we were going to our new location."

"We will be, eventually, but I thought we should make a stop first. We'll go in through a rear entrance."

Julia should be used to secretiveness, but she wasn't. She didn't know what to expect and she didn't want any more surprises, yet she dutifully followed Jonathan and guided her children through a heavy fire door and down a long tiled corridor. Stacy and Karl followed them.

Jonathan stopped in front of an elevator. The doors opened. He pushed the button, and once the two other marshals entered, standing a bit too close, the elevator rose a number of floors. When the doors opened, they stepped into another corridor.

"The children can wait in here," Jonathan said, motioning them into a waiting room. "This officer will escort you."

Julia didn't understand, but she was too tired to argue.

The children settled on a couch and closed their eyes. Stacy and Karl sat nearby.

"How long will I be gone?" she asked Jonathan.

"You can come back at any time," he assured her. "You'll just be down the hall."

She followed the police officer, not sure of where they were going or what she needed to see. He stopped at the third door on the right. She glanced back at the room where the three marshals remained with the children.

The officer pushed open the door and motioned her forward. Then he closed the door behind her.

Her heart stopped. The push and pull of machines sounded in the otherwise still hospital room. A curtain was drawn halfway to provide some semblance of privacy for the patient lying on the bed.

Julia moved silently forward and peered around the curtain, unwilling to believe what she saw.

His eyes blinked open.

"Abraham," she gasped, reaching for his hand and pulling it to her heart. "You're alive."

"Jul…ia."

Tears clouded her view. She wiped them away, unwilling to have anything keep her from seeing him for herself.

"The surgery?"

He nodded ever so slightly. "Okay… I will…be…okay."

She laughed through her tears and rubbed her hand over his forehead. "I thought we had lost you."

"I lived…for you."

His words brought joy to her heart. "And I didn't want to live without you. I knew I had to go on because of the children, but there was nothing left."

"I…I need you, Julia."

"Oh, Abraham."

"I want us to be together…you…me…the children."

"That's what I want, too."

"I..." He struggled to make his voice heard. "I love you and want...to be with you...for the rest of my life."

"Oh, Abraham."

"I...will love...you...forever, Julia."

She lowered her lips to his for one sweet kiss that she wanted to last for a lifetime.

When their lips parted, she sighed. "I love you, Abraham. Sleep now, so you can get stronger."

His eyes closed, but Julia remained at his side, holding his hand and giving thanks that the man she loved was alive.

TWENTY-FOUR

Julia's stomach was a tumble of nerves that had her running to the window every few minutes. She smiled, thinking of Kayla's admonishment back in Yoder that a watched pot never boiled. Today Julia's proverbial pot wasn't even lukewarm, yet she couldn't sit still so she paced back and forth across the kitchen, grateful for this home and the new Amish community that had welcomed her and her children. In the six weeks since they had arrived, the children had made friends and had started to sink roots. The only thing missing was Abraham.

His surgery had been successful, but his recovery had been long and complicated, marred by a secondary infection that had extended his time in rehab.

She looked around the house to ensure everything was tidy and in its place. The schoolbooks for the children were on the shelf, the sewing she had been working on was folded and put in a chest near her treadle machine, and her Bible—the book she so dearly loved to read each morning when she rose and each evening before sleep—sat on the small table near her rocking chair.

Over the last six weeks, she had fully embraced the Amish faith. The local bishop was pleased with her progress. Julia was, as well.

Her baptism in the not-too-distant future would be another turning point. She had experienced so many over the last two months—the Philadores' break-in, the flight to Kansas, meeting Abraham and having her life change forever. Now, a new identity in a small Amish community in Ohio.

William had testified. Fuentes had been brought to justice and would remain incarcerated for the rest of his life. The gang that had done so much harm was crumbling without his leadership and, hopefully someday, would be only a painful memory of how young men could seek affirmation and a sense of belonging in the wrong way.

Her hand touched the sideboard, the wood smooth under her fingers. She pulled open the drawer. The letter lay there. Charlie had written both children. In his tight script, he had asked their forgiveness for not being a good father and for the mistakes he had made.

Somehow the sealed envelope had ended up in Jonathan's hands. He had brought it to her on his last visit. Not knowing what it might contain, she had been hesitant at first, but with her new ability to trust the ways of the Lord, she had given it to the children. The letter had started the healing process both of them needed.

Charlie had sent a separate note to Julia, taking full responsibility for their failed marriage. "I didn't know what it meant to be a husband or father," he had written. "The prison chaplain said, in truth, we never had a valid marriage because I didn't know how to love." The note brought comfort and removed the last traces of guilt she had carried for so long.

A car sounded in the drive. Her pulse raced. She closed the drawer and pulled in a deep breath. As footsteps sounded on the porch, she threw open the door.

Her heart nearly pounded out of her chest when she beheld the man standing there. "Oh, Abraham."

Without saying a word, he opened his arms. She fell into his embrace, mindful of his still-fragile wounds.

"I have missed you, Julia."

Her heart soared.

He had lost weight in his ordeal, but he was still the strong man who had protected her and her children.

"Come inside." She motioned him forward, then glancing at the car idling in the driveway, she waved to the driver. "The *dawdy* house next door is open. Leave his bags there."

"Thanks so much," Abraham called to the driver after he had delivered the bags.

"You're staying in the house next door," Julia explained. "It's one story, so you don't have to worry about stairs."

"I can climb stairs, Julia."

"No farm work yet, Jonathan told me. William is handling most of the difficult jobs. He could use your guidance."

"And Kayla?" he asked.

"She's eager to see you. The children went to town with a neighbor. I wanted to get the house ready and have you to myself for a few minutes, knowing they wouldn't let you out of their sight once you arrived."

The car pulled out of the drive and Julia closed the door, then took Abraham's hand. "You could have gone home to Yoder, but Jonathan said you chose to come here and recuperate with us."

"I sold the farm, Julia. The youngest of Harvey Raber's three sons bought the place. From what I have learned, the oldest son has been attentive to Sarah. The matchmakers in the area are anticipating a wedding after harvest this fall."

"Sarah deserves a good man."

"You do, too, Julia."

Her heart fluttered. "I have a good man, Abraham, a man who is trustworthy and caring, hardworking and who loves the Lord. Why would I look for another?"

He touched her *kapp* and smiled. "Jonathan said you are meeting with the bishop."

She nodded. "I still struggle with the *heute deutsch* and the Pennsylvania Dutch, but he assures me that will come with time. He has not questioned my desire to be baptized."

"Once you become truly Amish, Julia, all the men in the area will come courting."

She laughed. "Oh, Abraham, if they look into my eyes they will know that I have given my heart to another."

"Should I be jealous?" His mouth curved into a playful smile.

"Maybe a little," she teased.

"I love you, Julia."

He lowered his lips to hers and time stood still as they melded together. Never had she felt such a sense of completion.

He pulled back ever so slightly.

The seriousness of his gaze threw her off balance.

"Is something wrong?" she asked.

"Not wrong, just unfinished."

She raised her brow.

"I want more than the *dawdy* house, Julia. I want to be with you and the children in our own house. I want to wake each morning knowing you will be there and that together we will face the day and whatever it brings. I want to be your husband and care for you and protect you as best I can, and to love you and cherish you for the rest of my life."

"Oh, Abraham. I want that, as well."

"You will marry me, Julia?" he asked.

"Yes! It's what I've wanted for so long."

"And the children?"

"They already think of you as their father, their *datt*. Kayla gave her doll to a little girl who had recently lost her father. Kayla said she didn't need Annie anymore."

Abraham was visibly touched by the child's thoughtfulness. "I told you about the boy who was kidnapped years ago?"

Julia nodded. "He was the reason you became a police officer."

"Which is what I always thought. But in the hospital, I realized the little boy I wanted to save was really me, although I never knew what I needed to make my life whole. Not until you and the children came into my world."

"Oh, Abraham, I love you."

They kissed and then kissed again and again until a buggy turned into the drive and the sound of children's laughter filled the air. Julia opened the door. Abraham bent down and Kayla ran into his arms.

"Careful, Kayla, of his side," Julia cautioned.

"Mr. Abraham, *Mamm* said you would be here when we came back from town. I did not think the buggy would go fast enough." She wrapped her arms around his neck and kissed his cheek, her face aglow.

"You have gotten so big, Kayla," he said.

"And I help *Mamm*. Now I can bake cookies almost by myself, and I'm studying hard so I can be a teacher."

He kissed her cheek, then stood and looked toward the door where William waited, as if not sure what to say.

"When did you grow up, William?" Abraham asked, the pride evident in his tone.

"I still have a lot to learn."

"*Yah*, and I have a lot to teach you. Come here. Let me wrap my arms around you, son."

The invitation was all William needed. His smile was almost wider than his face as he stepped into Abraham's embrace.

Kayla pushed between them and Julia stepped closer, her heart bursting with joy as she stretched her arms around the family she loved.

Later, when the children were doing their afternoon chores and dinner simmered on the stove, Julia sat with Abraham, their hands entwined.

"Have you talked to Jonathan recently about the Philadores?" she asked.

"Without Fuentes, they seem to have lost their edge."

"Does that mean William is truly safe?"

"For now, especially living here. Are you sure you do not want to go back to your old way of life, Julia?"

She shook her head. "I have found everything I have ever wanted, Abraham, living Amish. There was only one thing I was missing."

He raised a brow.

"You."

She snuggled closer and turned her lips to his. They would face the future together. Abraham would always be her protector, her husband and her friend.

Someday they would have children of their own. Kayla would be big sister. William would help Abraham with the livestock and the farm and learn to take on more responsibilities as he grew.

Jonathan had mentioned helping other families who would need new identities to escape crime. Julia trusted

God would reveal who needed their assistance and support in the future. Right now, she was only interested in the present moment with Abraham by her side. What else could she want? She had everything and more, her children, her faith and a wonderful man who filled her heart with love.

* * * * *

If you enjoyed Amish Safe House,
look for the thrilling conclusion to the
Amish Witness Protection series,
Amish Haven
by Dana R. Lynn.

Dear Reader,

I hope you enjoyed *Amish Safe House*, Book 2 in the Amish Witness Protection continuity. In this story, Julia Bradford's son witnesses a gang murder, and she and her two children are forced into witness protection. They find refuge with Abraham King. The reclusive former cop, now living Amish, lost his wife and child tragically to violence three years earlier. If he couldn't protect them, how will he be able to protect Julia and her family now? They're in danger of losing their lives while Abraham is in danger of losing his heart.

I pray for my readers each day and would love to hear from you. Email me at debby@debbygiusti.com, write me c/o Love Inspired, 195 Broadway, 24th Floor, New York, NY 10007 or visit me at www.DebbyGiusti.com and at www.facebook.com/debby.giusti.9.

As always, I thank God for bringing us together through this story.

Wishing you abundant blessings,
Debby

COMING NEXT MONTH FROM
Love Inspired® Suspense

Available March 5, 2019

AMISH HAVEN
Amish Witness Protection • by Dana R. Lynn

When criminal lawyer Tyler Everson witnesses a murder, he becomes the killer's next target—along with his estranged wife, Annabelle, and their daughter. Now they must enter witness protection in Amish country. But will going into hiding keep them safe...and bring the family back together?

DANGEROUS SANCTUARY
FBI: Special Crimes Unit • by Shirlee McCoy

FBI agent Radley Tumberg must rescue his fellow agent, Honor Remington, from a spiritual sanctuary where she's being held against her will. But when he reaches her, can they work together to escape the sanctuary and find evidence that its leader isn't what he's pretending to be?

BURIED MOUNTAIN SECRETS
by Terri Reed

While searching for her missing brother in the mountains near their home, Maya Gallo finds herself caught between treasure hunters and the bounty they'll kill for. But with help from mounted patrol deputy Alex Trevino, she might be able to save her brother...and stay alive.

MURDER MIX-UP
by Lisa Phillips

After a man is killed while carrying a navy ID belonging to Secret Service agent Declan Stringer's brother, Declan is determined to figure out why. Even if it means turning a killer's sights on him...and convincing NCIS agent Portia Finch he'd make a great temporary partner.

INNOCENT TARGET
by Elisabeth Rees

Journalist Kitty Linklater knows her father isn't a murderer, and she plans to prove it—especially after the town turns on her and someone becomes determined to silence her. Chief Deputy Ryan Lawrence doesn't believe in her father's innocence, but he'll risk his life to guard her.

SHATTERED TRUST
by Sara K. Parker

After Natalie Harper was left at the altar, enjoying her honeymoon alone is the best way to cope—until she's attacked on the beach. Luke Everett, the bodyguard hired by her federal judge father, arrives just in time to ensure she survives. But can he figure out why the assailant's after her?

LOOK FOR THESE AND OTHER LOVE INSPIRED BOOKS WHEREVER BOOKS ARE SOLD, INCLUDING MOST BOOKSTORES, SUPERMARKETS, DISCOUNT STORES AND DRUGSTORES.

LISCNM0219

Annie was cleaning up the dishes when the phone rang. She didn't recognize the number.

"Hello?"

"Annie, it's me."

Tyler.

Her estranged husband. The man she hadn't seen in two years.

"Annie? You there?"

She shook her head. "Yes, I'm here. It's been a frazzling day, Tyler. What do you want?"

A pause. "Something's happened last night, Annie. I can't tell you everything, but the US Marshals are involved. I'm being put into witness protection."

"Witness protection? Tyler, people in those programs have to completely disappear."

In her mind, she heard Bethany ask when she would see her daddy again.

"I know. It won't be forever. At least I hope it won't. I need to testify against someone. Maybe after that, I can go back to being me."

A sudden thought occurred to her. "Tyler, the reason you're going into witness protection… Would it affect me at all?"

"What do you mean?"

"Someone was following me today."

"Someone's following you?" Tyler exclaimed, horrified.

"You never answered. Could the man following me be related to what happened to you?"

"I don't know. Annie, I will call you back." He disconnected the call and went down the hall.

Marshal Mast was sitting at a laptop in an office at the back of the house. He glanced up from the screen as Tyler entered. "Something on your mind, Tyler?"

"I called my wife to tell her I was going into witness protection. She said she and my daughter were being followed today."

At this information, Jonathan Mast jumped to his feet. "Karl!"

Feet pounded in the hallway. Marshal Karl Adams entered the room at a brisk pace. "Jonathan? Did you need me?"

"Yes, I need you to make a trip for me. What's the address, Tyler?"

Tyler recited the address. Would Karl and Stacy get there in time? How he wished he could go with him…